Home Remedies

Home Remedies

ANGELA PNEUMAN

A HARVEST ORIGINAL
HARCOURT, INC.
Orlando   Austin   New York   San Diego   Toronto   London

www.HarcourtBooks.com

The following stories have previously appeared elsewhere:
"Home Remedies" in *The New England Review;* "All Saints' Day" in
The Virginia Quarterly Review and *The Best American Short Stories 2004;*
"The Bell Ringer" in *Glimmer Train;* "Invitation" in *Puerto del Sol;*
"The Beachcomber" in *StoryQuarterly;* "Holy Land" in
The Los Angeles Review; "The Long Game" in *Ploughshares.*

Library of Congress Cataloging-in-Publication Data
Pneuman, Angela.
Home remedies/Angela Pneuman.—1st ed.
p. cm.
"A Harvest original."
I. Title.
PS3616.N48 2006
813'.54—dc22 2006007670
ISBN-13: 978-0-15-603075-5 ISBN-10: 0-15-603075-6

Text set in Perpetua
Designed by Linda Lockowitz

First edition
Printed in the United States of America

A C E G I K J H F D B

All those girls
who wore the red shoes,
each boarded a train that would not stop.

ANNE SEXTON, "THE RED SHOES"

Contents

Home Remedies

When Lena gets sick, June, her mother, doesn't notice for two days. It's a Kentucky January, bleak and rainy with an occasional paltry snow, and Lena's father, Patrick, from whom June has been divorced one year, has just announced his plans to remarry in March. Lena hears her mother talking to friends on the phone, her voice cheery and capable. "Oh, well, you know, it was bound to happen. We're both moving on. Now, six months ago? I would have been shaken to the core." But off the phone, June shifts around the house, teary-eyed at irrelevant things she brings to Lena's attention: a greeting-card commercial on television, the few dead leaves still stuck to the branches of the sycamore outside the kitchen window, a lumpy ceramic turtle Lena made for Patrick in kindergarten, four years ago. To cheer up, June gives herself a home perm, and her hair turns frazzly, separating into kinky hunks with straight, brittle ends. "What do you think?" June says, holding up the back of her hair with her hand, lowering her head for Lena to see.

Lena squeezes a fistful, says it feels like the pink roof insulation in the attic. This sends June to her bedroom for an hour.

At school Lena sits at her desk, listless and warm. The glands at the back of her throat swell to the size of peas, and when her teacher takes the class to the bathrooms, Lena pushes past the other girls to the mirrors over the sink, where under the fluorescent light she tries to see. She opens her mouth so wide that the corners crack into tiny grains of dry skin, but her throat lies in shadow. All day she probes the lumps with the back of her tongue, just to make sure they're still sore. She likes how her voice has gone husky.

At home June circles the wedding date, March twelfth, with a red pen on the calendar by the refrigerator. Since the announcement she's been talking to the pastor each week again, as she did just after the divorce, and has taken to repeating for Lena phrases he gives her: "You must learn to love yourself," and "All things work together for good."

"I want you to fully grasp that," she tells Lena. It's easy, she's said on the phone, to talk to Lena as though the girl is much older. It could have something to do with how Lena's eyes shrink behind thick glasses, how in sickness her skin has taken on a yellowish tint.

"Do you love yourself, Lena?" June asks, bringing her face so close that Lena can see every hair, every pore. This close, faces look like something else entirely, the nubbly surface of the planets Lena's seen on science shows.

"I guess," says Lena. She's never thought about feeling

anything at all for herself, as though she were another person, but June seems to think it's important, which means it might be or it might not be. The problem with June, Lena once heard Patrick say, is that everything turns into a big production. A weepy federal case.

"What's that you're doing with your mouth?" June says.

Lena has been feeling her glands, and she bites her tongue to keep it still. On her hot forehead, June's palm is clammy.

"You're burning up, Lena. You're hot as can be. Have you been feeling bad?"

"I can feel my throat," Lena says.

"You're sick," June says. "Lena, you're sick. I didn't notice and you didn't say. Why didn't you say? You have to say, Lena." June's fingers disappear into her stiff hair. She closes her eyes and says, "I feel like a horrible mother."

IT TURNS OUT TO BE strep throat. June takes off from work, the doctor gives Lena some medicine, and after four days and a weekend Lena returns to school. But three weeks later, she's sick again. This happens sometimes, the doctor says. If the antibiotic doesn't kill all the bacteria, they come back with renewed force. Lena pictures it like tug-of-war in gym. All the bacteria on one team, lunging hard to make their comeback.

June is in a pinch. She processes payments at the electric company and has run out of days she can take off. The woman who used to sit for Lena during the day now has two toddlers of her own, and won't expose them to strep.

All the mothers of Lena's friends work, the teenaged girls are in school, and Patrick lives half a day away, over the border into Tennessee. So the pastor makes an announcement at church about a member needing a sitter, and the following Monday morning Mrs. Shefferd arrives. She is a small, bony woman, with short hair gone completely white, and she wears a faux leopard-print coat from Sears, some thirty years old. Because it doesn't button all the way, Mrs. Shefferd wears a jacket underneath, and several sweaters underneath the jacket.

"Lena, back to bed," June says. She clips earrings onto her earlobes and buttons her own coat. "Mrs. Shefferd, I've left directions on the counter."

"Go on, now," says Mrs. Shefferd, her voice throaty and sure. "You don't worry about a thing."

Each morning when Lena wakes up, Mrs. Shefferd greets her with a glass of water. The directions say for Lena to drink a glass of water each hour, even though after the fourth glass, fourth hour, she can hear her stomach sloshing and has to pee every ten minutes. The directions also say when the antibiotic is to be taken and what Lena is to have for lunch each day. The notes make it clear Lena should stay in bed, but Mrs. Shefferd allows her to lie on the couch in the front room and watch television. Mrs. Shefferd rocks purposefully in June's antique rocking chair, the one Lena's supposed to be careful of. During commercials she asks Lena questions. Not the questions Lena has come to expect from old ladies—nothing about school, or church, or her parents. Instead, Mrs. Shefferd offers choices. "Where would you rather live," she asks, "the beach or the mountains?" Lena says "beach" and Mrs. Shefferd reminds her of hurricanes and tidal waves. Lena says "mountains" and Mrs. Shefferd reminds her, cheerfully, that some mountains are volcanoes.

"If you could only eat foods that begin with 'r' or 'c,'" Mrs. Shefferd says, "which would you pick?"

"R," Lena says.

"No celery? No Cream of Wheat?"

"I like roast beef," Lena says.

"Oh, yes, and rhubarb and rutabaga," says Mrs. Shefferd. "Good thinking."

When Lena feels like being up and around, she drags projects out from the back of her closet—crocheting that her grandmother tried to teach her on the last visit, a half-finished floral paint-by-number, the oils gone slick and runny inside their tiny plastic vials. Mrs. Shefferd comments politely on the painting and fingers the crocheting—just a granny square in tricolor pink yarn that Lena can't even remember how she made.

"I don't know how to crochet," Mrs. Shefferd says. She holds the square to the lamp, then rubs it against her face, eyes closed. "My mother was a different breed." Lena, kneeling at her feet, can smell cinnamon on Mrs. Shefferd's breath. On the television people exclaim and jump around, having won a prize for guessing something, but Lena has turned down the sound.

Lena brings out her shoebox of teeth from her father's office of orthodontics. They aren't real, are really just the molds he makes of patients' teeth, to display on before-and-after shelves in the waiting room and to take to conferences. These are the leftovers, and Lena lines them up on the living room floor for Mrs. Shefferd to admire, which she does; so many sets of jaws, incisors twisted in their sockets, or pushed into unnatural rows, and plaster gums that just end, the irregular shapes of upper mouths. There are also strips of wax in little boxes, miniature rubber bands of all colors that Lena and Mrs. Shefferd string on yarn for necklaces, and a black mouthpiece Lena's father uses to wedge open his patients' mouths, and to pin down their tongues. It's a durable plastic, so that if the hand of his assistant slips, or even his own—though this has never happened—and nicks a tongue or gouges the inside of a cheek with a wire, the plastic piece keeps the patient's jaw from clamping shut on anyone's fingers.

In the bathroom Lena and Mrs. Shefferd angle a flashlight so that Lena can see her throat in the mirror. Mrs. Shefferd points with the wrong end of a toothbrush. "Those are the glands you can feel," she says, indicating red nodules behind her teeth. They look smaller than they feel on Lena's tongue. Her throat and the inside of her mouth are all slimy pink, shot through with tiny purple veins. "And those," Mrs. Shefferd says, pointing just behind the first pair, "are your tonsils." Lena strains toward the light. The tonsils look like red raisins embedded in the veiny surface.

MRS. SHEFFERD FROWNS when she doles out the antibiotic before making lunch. "It's not what they think," she says, standing over Lena at the table. "These make you weak. Next time you'll need more to do the same thing, mark my words."

Lena feels the capsule on the back of her tongue. Just last year she had to have syrup because she gagged, but now she can swallow a pill without flinching, though she feels its shadow in her throat for a minute afterward, no matter how much water she drinks.

"My mother would have done something different," Mrs. Shefferd says. "I'm not criticizing. Your mother does the best she can. She's good with the water. It flushes out your system."

For lunch Mrs. Shefferd heats canned soup, or spreads peanut butter and jelly. One day she makes toast, because that's what Lena wants, even though it's not specified in the directions. Mrs. Shefferd makes toast in the skillet, with butter, instead of in the toaster. Fried toast. Lena, who hasn't been eating well, eats twelve pieces. Mrs. Shefferd has six or seven, and then toasts the heels of the bread for dessert. When June comes home, she asks what happened to all the bread, but Lena just shrugs.

AFTER THE WEDDING announcement, June begins to appear beside Lena's bed in the middle of the night. "Lena," she says, shaking her awake. "Lena, we need to talk about your father getting married again. You're upset, I know. You can tell me how you really feel. What do you think of Mandy?"

June sits on the edge of the bed, looking fuzzy around the edges to Lena, whose glasses are on the dresser. On her lap June holds a handful of white Kleenex, which glow from the streetlight shining through the window.

"She's fine," Lena says, yawning.

"You can tell me," June says.

"She's fine," Lena says again. Mandy has a convertible, and at Christmas she put the top down and took Lena for a drive, even though it was only forty degrees out. Mandy likes country music and taught Lena the two-step. Mandy makes muscles in her own thighs and slaps at them, trying to see any jiggle.

"I know it's confusing," June says. "This is such a diffi-cult time for both of us."

"Are you going to cry?" Lena asks. She likes to know in advance so she can prepare herself. The first few times she saw June cry, right after Patrick left, Lena just sat there watching until June said, through tears, "Could you hug me, do you think? Would that be such a chore?"

When Lena hugged her, too late, she discovered that June didn't smell the way she used to smell. She used to smell like lotion and the wind, but she'd begun to smell like coffee and dirty hair, even though she washed her hair every day.

"I don't know," says June now. "I might cry, I might not."

Lena can hear in June's voice that it was the wrong thing to ask.

"Would that be okay with you, Lena, if I happened to cry about something? Do you think you could tolerate that? If I happened to feel bad enough about something to cry?" June has indeed begun to cry, with her eyes open, looking at Lena while the tears gather and spill out.

"You can cry," Lena says. She feels achy in the back of her neck.

"Oh, thank you," says June. "Thank you, Lena, for your permission. I try not to burden you with my problems." She's stopped crying.

For a few moments they are silent. Lena closes her eyes. She memorizes where each thing in her room is. Her dresser under the window, her bookcase beside the bed, her trunk with the extra blankets and her summer clothes. She pictures the lamp on the dresser, the framed photos of her mother, father, and grandmother on top of the bookcase. She thinks that if she were blind she might be able to make it around the room just fine, locating each and every thing from memory, never running into corners or forgetting where she put something.

"Lena?" June says.

Lena opens her eyes.

"What were you thinking?"

"I don't know," Lena says.

"Just now. Tell me what you were thinking." June is looking at her closely.

"I can't remember," Lena says.

"Do you miss Daddy?" June asks, mangling the word "Daddy" with a special emphasis.

"I don't know," Lena says. June has asked this before, but the way things are now gets in the way of what Lena remembers. She talks to Patrick on the phone every other week, and it seems so long since he lived with them that Lena can't imagine things any other way.

"Were you thinking about Daddy?" June asks, wincing again at the word. She is working the Kleenex with her fingers, wadding them into a tiny ball.

"I was thinking what if I was blind."

"And?" June's hands stop.

"That's it," says Lena.

MRS. SHEFFERD TELLS Lena that her mother's name was Harriet, but everyone called her Hat, even Mrs. Shefferd.

"She was fearless," says Mrs. Shefferd. "Against her parents' wishes, she ran off with a boy just discharged from the army. She was a Kentucky girl, like you, and only fifteen years old, and she ran with him all the way to Sandwich, New Hampshire, where they married."

They're standing by the kitchen sink. Mrs. Shefferd runs hot water into a glass and stirs in salt for Lena to gargle.

The boy's name was Henry, though Mrs. Shefferd heard Hat say it only once, years later. While Lena gargles, Mrs. Shefferd tells her how Hat loved him fiercely for over two years. Then how, during their third winter, she and Henry went out onto Squam Lake to the fishing hole hacked into the thinner ice out toward the middle, a rough circle about the size of a washtub. They set up their poles and Hat wandered off about fifty yards to watch a group of skaters scraping a patch of ice smooth with shovels. Then she watched them show each other how to spin, thick as bears in their bulky clothes, but graceful, too. Out there on the lake, under a low gray sky indistinguishable from the cloudy ice, it was easy to lose time, and when Hat turned to go back to her husband, she saw only their fishing gear, their tin lunch-box, and the burlap sack they'd brought to sit on. At the time she'd been a month pregnant with Mrs. Shefferd, but she didn't know it yet. Hat cried out and ran, skidding in her boots, toward the hole. She plunged into the frigid, dark water, where she remained submerged for a full minute, looking for him, before the skaters pulled her out.

The skaters didn't have to look for Henry. They'd seen him leave. Over by the shore, where the ice could get up to ten feet thick, there'd been a young woman learning to drive her father's Model A Ford. She'd been tracing a fig-ure eight, and Henry had gone over to have a look at the engine. The skaters said he'd traced a couple of figure eights with her, then they drove right off the ice and onto the road, and, Hat found out later, kept driving to Manchester, where they lived together for years.

Lena spits the last of the salt water into the sink. Out-side in the yard the snow has melted in muddy patches. She thinks of the nearest body of water, a reservoir across town that freezes only halfway, and that only twice or so a winter.

Pinned to her collar, Mrs. Shefferd wears a small plastic turkey left over from Thanksgiving. She reaches up and presses something on the turkey, and the part of its body with the feathers falls open to reveal a circle of Vaseline inside.

"Hat just dove in after him," Mrs. Shefferd says, ab-sently spreading Vaseline onto her lips, offering some to

Lena. "Of course he turned out to be no-'count, but she thought nothing of risking life and limb. That's just the way she was."

That night June comes home with a beauty magazine and gives herself a facial in the bathroom. She emerges once, towel wrapped around her head like a turban, and boils water on the stove to melt the wax she uses on her upper lip.

Lena sits at the kitchen table, working makeup multiplication problems from school. "If you're going to drown," she asks June, "which do you think is better, freezing water or warm water?"

"Drowning," June says. She lowers the jar with the yellow wax into the boiling water. "Where have you heard about drowning?"

"Freezing is best," says Lena. "Your body can freeze and you can go unconscious and still live on the oxygen you already have, because you need less oxygen anyway, when you're unconscious."

"Honestly, Lena," June says.

"But if you're in warm water, or even if you're in cold, and instead of letting yourself freeze, you keep trying to breathe and stay afloat, then your lungs fill up with water."

"I told Mrs. Shefferd to pay attention to what was on television. I don't like for you to watch those scary movies."

"It wasn't a movie. Mrs. Shefferd told me."

"Does Mrs. Shefferd make whole lists of preferable ways to die?"

"You don't die if you freeze first," says Lena. "I just told you about the oxygen."

"Mrs. Shefferd should be taken with a grain of salt," June says. She lifts the pan off the burner, grabs the jar of wax with a hot mitt, and disappears into the bathroom.

Soon Lena has to pee, but she waits as long as she can. When she finally knocks at the door, June has taken off her shirt and bra, and has packed a mud mask on her neck and upper chest. She's been crying again—her eyes are puffy. People often say June is pretty, but at the moment her face is mottled with red fingernail prints from where she's squeezed at the tiny blemishes that hardly even showed before she started. The skin above her lip is a red strip, and she's plucked one eyebrow almost clean away.

"Can I pee?" Lena asks.

"Go ahead," says June.

"In front of you?"

"Yes, in front of me," June says. "I am your mother. It is okay for us to see each other naked."

June is in the habit of commenting on Lena's body, on the future, when Lena will grow pubic hair and breasts. On June's breasts, everything slopes down to large brown nipples, surrounded by circles of brown gooseflesh. At the thought of anything on her body resembling these, Lena shudders.

"I don't have to go anymore," she says. June's stomach rolls just a tiny bit where it meets her skirt. Without a bra, her nipples point to the left and right instead of straight ahead.

"Lena, come in here and pee. Come in here and pee right now, with me standing at the sink. It won't kill you."

"I don't have to, anymore," Lena says. She backs away.

June sighs. She rests her fists on either edge of the counter, her head down, looking into the sink like she's expecting something to bubble up out of the drain.

Lena hovers in the hall in case June changes her mind.

"You're shutting me out," June finally says, stepping out into the hall. "You're resentful and you're shutting me out. But what did I do, Lena? I didn't want any of this."

"Any of what?" Lena says. She crosses her legs in front of her. "I just have to pee."

MRS. SHEFFERD TELLS Lena how Hat stayed on in the area, birthing Mrs. Shefferd almost by herself—going just by the feel of it; she'd never had children before—just telling the neighbor woman where to grip and pull. After Mrs. Shefferd was born, Hat delivered most of the babies in town. She liked to cut umbilical cords with a special curved knife she made herself by taking apart a pair of haircutting scissors and heating one of the blades, bending it to a curve. She originally made the knife for digging out potato eyes, but it was the first thing handy when Mrs. Shefferd came out. Hat liked how the dipping motions of a curved blade needed less resistance than cutting with a straight one. Mrs. Shefferd demonstrates this for Lena, holding her fingers in front of Lena's face and making tiny scooping motions with her thumb.

"She cut the cords herself?" Lena asks.

"Oh, yes," says Mrs. Shefferd. "And when I was old enough to go with her, she let me do it. We kept the blade sharp and sterilized and wrapped in cotton in case we had to rush out anywhere. We did other things, too."

"What other things?" Lena asks. She lowers herself into a chair at the kitchen table while Mrs. Shefferd puts water on the stove for tea.

"Oh, this and that. We dug warts, pulled infected teeth. We cut off two sixth toes in the same family."

Lena glances down at her feet and wiggles her toes. When the kettle whistles, Mrs. Shefferd pours water into two of June's coffee cups, over tea bags she brings from home. She sits across the table from Lena and pushes a cup toward her. "Hat was very inventive," she says thoughtfully. "I remember what she did with this growth she had, once." Mrs. Shefferd gestures vaguely toward her stomach.

"Growth?" Lena imagines a sudden sprouting, something the yellow gray color of mucus.

"She pulled up her shirt and I saw it," Mrs. Shefferd says. "Sitting right there like a knob on the outside of her stomach. Like a kernel of hominy. Do you know hominy?"

Lena shakes her head. She feels in the back of her throat for her glands, but the swelling has mostly gone down. She is almost better, even though for the past two days she has gone without her antibiotic, miming the swallowing and retrieving the pill with her fingers to flush down the toilet.

"Hominy's a kind of cracked corn," says Mrs. Shefferd. "Bigger than a pea, smaller than popcorn. These days you get it in a can." Outside, the sun has come out. In the new light, Mrs. Shefferd blinks, remembering. Her eyes are green, and the right has a brown spot, directly under the pupil. She begins to brush crumbs off the vinyl place mat in front of her, collecting them in the palm of her hand.

"Hat called to me from the bedroom. 'Come here, Irene,' she said. I went to her, and she was lying on the bed, propped up on the pillow." Mrs. Shefferd sips her tea. "Beside the bed Hat had a spool of white thread. The strong cotton kind for buttons and quilting. I sat beside her and she made a little loop with the thread"—Mrs. Shefferd makes an invisible loop over her tea—"and she fastened the loop onto the growth. A tiny noose."

Something thrills in Lena's stomach. She keeps her eyes on her fingernails. In bed the night before, she painted her nails pink, and now she bends the tips so that the polish cracks. She has her mother's weak nails.

Mrs. Shefferd describes the twisting of the thread like a tourniquet in miniature, Hat's hands gripping a spool in the pine headboard. When it finally came off, Mrs. Shefferd says, the growth, it really came out. It had a root.

"Root?" Lena says.

Mrs. Shefferd measures an inch on her finger with her thumb. "It looked like a bean sprout," she says, "but thicker. A plug."

"Did it bleed?" asks Lena.

"Not much," says Mrs. Shefferd.

"Did it hurt?" asks Lena.

"Oh, yes," says Mrs. Shefferd. "But Hat was no stranger to pain."

WHEN JUNE COMES HOME, Lena has invited Mrs. Shefferd for dinner. She tells June this in front of Mrs. Shefferd, who has already accepted.

"Oh, Mrs. Shefferd," June says. "I'm sure you already have dinner plans."

"No," says Mrs. Shefferd. She stands beside the coat tree, where her leopard coat and sweaters hang, but she makes no move to put them on.

"We don't have much in the refrigerator," June tries again. At the electric company she is on the phone for a good part of the day, and her voice still sounds professional, lilting and steely. Often when someone calls in the evenings to ask her to do something, she says she has to stay home with her daughter, who is sick. Lena has heard her say this even when she isn't sick. Dinner, June frequently tells Lena, is their together-time, and she doesn't like to have people in.

June tightens her mouth and lowers her eyes. It is clear she thinks that other adults should recognize when children have put their parents in uncomfortable situations. This is a situation to be excused by Mrs. Shefferd, to be gracefully bowed out of.

"I don't mind," says Mrs. Shefferd. "I was just going to whip up spaghetti at home."

June says, "Lena, I'll speak to you in the other room. Excuse us, Mrs. Shefferd."

In the kitchen, June sits down at the table. "Do you have any idea what I'm going through?" she asks Lena. "Do you?" June's hands shake a little—she has low blood sugar—and she rubs at her hairline with her fingertips. "Do not ever do this to me again," June hisses. Then she goes out to the living room and tells Mrs. Shefferd that it's not a good night, that it would be poor judgment to tire out Lena just when she's beginning to feel better.

"A rain check, then," says Mrs. Shefferd, loud enough for Lena to hear.

"Well, sure," says June. "We'll just have to see."

When Lena has been back in school for two weeks, June's boss, who is also divorced, invites them to Ringling Brothers Barnum & Bailey with him and his children. June sits next to her boss, and Lena sits wedged between a stranger and the boss's littlest boy, who cries out whenever the trapeze artists above let go their bars and swing and somersault through the air. Lena tells him to close his eyes, and he does, just as a clown slips and falls into the net below, on purpose, it seems to Lena, just to hear the crowd go, "Ooooooooh!" Lena does not like clowns, or even circuses, she discovers. The music gives her a headache. She thinks she feels the beginnings of a sore throat, but it could just be from the lemonade June's boss bought for her. She does like how the woman in tights puts her head inside the lion's jaws, but that part is quickly over.

Outside, on the way to the parking lot, they pass through

the snake house, where a man lowers live rats into each tank to be either eaten alive, digested by the pythons in rat-sized bulges, or to be struck with the fangs of cobras. "Yuck," says June, turning away. "What a choice." Lena leans in for a closer look. In one cage the man jerks the rat away from the cobra for the first few times, and the cobra's fangs hit the side of the glass tank, right in front of Lena's face.

"How did you like the circus?" June asks that night as they are brushing their teeth at the sink.

"How did *you* like the circus," Lena asks instead of answering. She tries to sound interested.

June spits into the sink, rinses, then stands her toothbrush back in the cup. She narrows her eyes. "No," she says. "You tell me if you liked it *before* you know whether I liked it or not. You're always waiting to see what you're supposed to say."

"I liked it," Lena says, but there's something in her voice she can't help.

"Say what you really think," June says.

Lena tries to pass her and go out into the living room, but June stops her.

"Sit down," she says. "We're not finished, here." She grabs Lena's shoulders and pushes her down so that she's sitting on the closed toilet lid. "You didn't like the circus?"

Lena shakes her head.

"What didn't you like about it?"

Lena shrugs.

"Did something unpleasant happen?"

"No."

"It isn't Gerald, is it?" June asks. Gerald is June's boss. He is a jowly, balding man who kept getting up for refreshments. "It wasn't really a date. You wouldn't like it if I started seeing someone, would you, Lena? Wouldn't that feel strange?"

Lena twists her mouth to the side, trying to feel strange about it. She pictures Gerald standing with her mother, helping her on with her coat, and wonders if this should bother her, but she doesn't feel anything.

"No," Lena says, finally.

"Don't just say what you think I want to hear," June says. Lena used to think June's eyes were blue, but they're gray now, almost the color of pavement, and this close the whites look like they're covered with a clear, silvery film.

"Lena?"

Lena reaches into the sink and turns the cold water on and off.

June closes her eyes and says, "Stop, please, with the water." She says, "Goddammit, Lena, I do my best. You said you wanted to go to the circus."

June had just brought home the tickets one day, without asking, but neither of them acknowledges this.

"I have a sore throat," Lena says.

THIS TIME THE DOCTOR says Lena's tonsils have to come out. It's the end of February, and the operation will be at the end of March, over spring break. Lena wakes up before

June leaves for work and hears her telling Mrs. Shefferd that the tonsils are diseased with strep, which sounds important.

"She'll go to the hospital?" Mrs. Shefferd asks.

"Well, where else?" says June. Patrick's wedding is less than two weeks away, and she has a short fuse.

The first few days of March are unusually warm, and daffodils push up in clumps under June's windows. In the afternoons Mrs. Shefferd and Lena open up the house and sit in the front room, drinking iced tea.

"Well, now," says Mrs. Shefferd. "This I can understand. That virus stuff, that bacteria stuff is over my head, but taking something out—that's progress. If only there wasn't the hospital."

Mrs. Shefferd sips her iced tea and rocks in the rocking chair, her toes leaving the floor each time the chair rocks back. "I'll never forgive myself for what happened to my own mother."

"Why?" Lena asks. "What happened to her?"

Mrs. Shefferd looks at Lena, who has sucked her lips flat between her teeth. "Oh, honey, there's nothing for you to worry about. I'm sure everything will be fine. They'll just lift out those tonsils smooth as can be, and you'll be back to normal."

"What happened to Hat?" Lena asks again.

Mrs. Shefferd closes her eyes. She rocks back and forth so long that Lena thinks she's rocked herself to sleep, but then she speaks.

"They took the stuffing out of her," says Mrs. Shefferd. "The neighbors found her on the floor after I'd been away for two days, visiting a girlfriend, and they took her to the hospital. The doctor said she had a bad womb, a tumor, and he operated and said maybe she'd be all right, and then again maybe the cancer had gone through her body. They gave her the morphine for the operation and right after. When she ran out of it, she couldn't stop talking how her stomach throbbed, how numb her hands and feet had been ever since she'd dove into that water years ago. In winter she complained about her joints, and when summer came the heat bothered her.

"I understood," says Mrs. Shefferd. "I figured she'd feel poorly, losing her womb. But Hat knew she was a shadow of her former self, and when she saw what she'd turned into, how every little thing bothered her if she didn't have the morphine, she got hold of some more, somehow, and did herself in."

"She killed herself?" Lena asks, holding her breath.

"Yes," says Mrs. Shefferd, rocking. "Yes she did. She rather'd died than live like that. But I can't say that would happen now. They don't even use morphine anymore, do they? And maybe she would have gone into herself like that anyway, I don't know. Plain old age does some funny things. That's nothing for you to worry about."

The sun is going down, and the breeze from the window begins to feel like winter again. "I don't want to go," Lena says. Something else—the seed of an idea—is germinating in the back of her mind.

June's car pulls into the driveway.

"I'm sure everything will be fine," says Mrs. Shefferd. "Your mother knows best."

In the darkening living room, they listen to June's heels clicking up the walk to the front door.

"You could do it," Lena says. Her voice feels small.

"Oh, now," says Mrs. Shefferd, modestly. It is too dark to see her expression, but after a pause she dabs at the corners of her eyes with her shirtsleeve. "Well, Lena, would you look at me," she says. "My goodness."

"Lena?" June passes by the window and peers inside. "Are these windows open?" Lena sits very still, and June moves on to the door.

"Brrr," she says upon entering. She switches on a lamp and glares at Mrs. Shefferd. "It's freezing in here, and Lena sick, too."

A WEEK BEFORE the wedding, Patrick makes a last-ditch phone call to ask if June will change her mind and let Lena attend. June has put her foot down about this from the start—it is just too much to ask, and besides, Lena is still sick and no thanks to Mandy's convertible. Now Lena has to have an operation. There is a long pause on the phone and June says yes, she knows strep is a bacteria, she's not stupid; but if riding around in the cold can't weaken someone's resistance, what can? She tells Patrick to call Lena during the day from now on, when she isn't home, and slams the phone into its cradle.

In the middle of the night, Lena wakes to find her

standing beside the bed. "Can I sleep with you?" June asks. "Like I did when you were little and scared of the dark?"

"I'm not scared," Lena says.

"I know." June crawls under the covers. Lena moves over as close to the wall as she can.

"I'm worried about you, Lena," June says. "You don't talk to me anymore." June speaks into the dark, and Lena pretends she's asleep.

"I know you're not asleep," June says. "When you're sick as much as you are, sometimes there's something else wrong. Sometimes people can make themselves sick by not feeling things."

"I feel things," Lena says. "I feel sleepy." She makes her voice sleepy, even though she is wide awake and tense.

June turns on her side and tries to spoon Lena, her breasts spreading thickly against Lena's back like they could melt onto her for good.

"I'm hot," Lena says, and June moves away.

"I don't want him to get married, either," June says. "I'm hurting, too."

"I don't care," Lena mumbles into her pillow.

"What? I didn't hear you."

"I don't care if he gets married," Lena says more clearly into the dark room.

"You're angry at him," June says. "You don't care what he does, now. Serves him right."

"Leave me alone." Lena presses her body into the wall. "It's not a federal case."

June is very quiet. In a few seconds the bed starts shaking gently, and Lena hears June gasp. In a few more seconds, she rises and returns to her own room, and Lena can hear her crying. After what seems like hours, the sobs die into little hiccups, and then June snores.

Lena's throat is hot. She creeps past June's bedroom to the bathroom to fill her bedside glass with water. On the way back, June has stopped snoring and seems to be flailing her body from one side of the bed to the other. Every few seconds she moans. Lena tiptoes to her room and sips her water.

She is drifting off to sleep when she feels the thunk of June falling out of bed.

"Lena?" June calls. Her voice is groggy.

Lena turns over. She can always say she didn't hear.

"Lena?" June calls again, and Lena gets out of bed.

In June's bedroom, Lena stands over the blurry, crumpled shape of her mother. June looks like the man in a story Lena read, the one whose own skeleton has turned against him. The doctor takes out all his bones and the man lives on as a shapeless, wiggling mound. Lena toes her mother's thin silk nightie. "Get up," she says.

"I'm sleeping," June says from the floor. "I'm still asleep."

"Get up," Lena says again. "Get up." Her own voice sounds to her like barking.

"Help me, Lena," June says, struggling to sit up. She reaches for Lena's hand.

"Please," Lena says, stepping backward. "Please just get up."

"Goddammit, Lena," June says, fully awake now. "Just give me your hand."

"No," Lena says. She has another word, something very bad. She cannot think of a word worse than the one in her mind, now on her lips. It's a word she's only heard one time, and even Patrick had stopped in the middle of a fight to apologize for it. It's that bad, and Lena doesn't even know why she wants to say it, but she can't stop herself. The sound has already filled her mouth.

"Cunt." She whispers, and even before June begins to whimper, Lena is chanting, "I'm sorry, I'm sorry, I'm sorry." She knows the thing to do is kneel on the floor beside June, comfort her, but June has shrunk in on herself, boneless still and smaller than life. Her nightie has bunched around her waist in a way that makes touching her impossible, and Lena creeps back to her own bed.

In the morning Mrs. Shefferd squirts teething gel onto a Q-tip and tells Lena to open her mouth.

"I borrowed this from the church nursery," Mrs. Shefferd says. "It'll numb things a bit. Your hands might jerk up and hit me. It's the body's natural reaction. You don't want my hands to slip."

Lena sits in a ladder-back chair by the stove. She winds her arms in and around the slats of the back so they can't jerk out, and she asks Mrs. Shefferd to bind her wrists together with the curtain ties.

It's early, yet; June's been gone only ten minutes. On the table sits Lena's goosenecked desk lamp with a 150-watt bulb adjusted to directly over her head. Mrs. Shefferd has also laid out the black plastic mouth wedge from Lena's father, a bottle of Jim Beam, and Hat's curved knife on a piece of sterile gauze. The front right burner of the stove glows red, and on it rests the heating tip of a stainless-steel ice pick, for cauterizing.

Mrs. Shefferd says they have to wait for the whiskey to take effect, for the teething gel to fully penetrate.

"It'll hurt," Mrs. Shefferd says. "It's not everyone who can do this."

Lena nods. The room begins to throb, from the whiskey. The light on the table burns into her eyes, but she finds she doesn't mind. When she swallows, her throat is a thousand needles, like her feet when they've gone to sleep.

Mrs. Shefferd is still talking. She's saying how one day, nearly six years after Hat dove into the ice after her husband, he came back. Mrs. Shefferd had been watching her dice potatoes for stew when the man knocked on the door.

"Who is it, Irene?" Hat called, and Irene led him into the kitchen.

When Hat looked up, her face stayed pleasant, but her hands slipped—she'd had poor circulation ever since the lake—and she cut off the tip of her left index finger. It was really no more than the top part of the outermost digit, halfway through the fingernail and hardly worth bothering about, though by that time doctors had become more successful at reconnecting appendages. In the instant before the blood rose up, Mrs. Shefferd saw the severed part right there on the cutting board with the potatoes, like a tiny cross-section of sausage. The man moved to help her, but Hat stopped him.

"Not one step closer," she said, holding out her bloody finger.

The man backed away.

Hat didn't even clean her finger. She said "damn," but not harshly, more like it was all just an inconvenience, and then she tilted up the hot iron pot from the stove with her right hand. Without even flinching she pressed the open part of her finger onto the bottom of the pot. Mrs. Shefferd heard it sizzle. So did Henry.

"Good Christ," he said. "Hat!"

Hat yelled, of course, but it was more like a triumphant battle yell than a yell of pain. Later was when Hat explained to Mrs. Shefferd about cauterizing a wound to stop the bleeding. She kept a salve on the finger and soon the shriveled skin on either side of the tip reconnected.

"What was it you wanted, Henry?" Hat said as she dipped her burnt finger into a cup of water, but Henry was gone.

Mrs. Shefferd stops and peers down at Lena. "How're we feeling?" she asks, and Lena blinks and nods. Mrs. Shefferd gently wedges the black plastic mouthpiece between Lena's teeth, and Lena leans back her head against the top slat of the chair. Mrs. Shefferd takes up her mother's blade and wipes it again on the gauze. Her left hand is cool and firm on Lena's forehead.

"Now," Lena says. Her mouth forced open, her tongue pinned down by the plastic piece, it almost doesn't sound like a word—but Mrs. Shefferd understands.

All Saints' Day

ORD WAS THAT THE missionary kid had a demon, though no one was supposed to know. The Boyd family was visiting East Winder only for the weekend, and already eight-year-old Prudence had heard it from her younger sister, Grace, who heard it from her new friend, Anna, whose father was going to cast it out. Prudence figured that a cast-out demon would look like a puddle of split-pea soup the size of a welcome mat, and that it would move around the room, blob-like, trying to absorb its way into people. Her own father, the Reverend Yancey Boyd, didn't believe in demons or in talking about demons, except to say he didn't believe in them, end of discussion.

"The demon made Ryan Kitter paint himself purple all over," Grace said.

"*All* over?" Prudence asked. "Even his privates?"

"That's how they found him," Grace said. She was six. "The paint dried up and he was crying because it hurt him to pee."

The girls stood in front of the mirror in the spare room at the Moberlys' house. It was the afternoon of November first, and that night there was an All Saints' Day party for kids at the First United Methodist, where the Reverend Yancey Boyd might be the new minister. Prudence was busy cutting a slit for Grace's head in a piece of old brown sheet. Everyone had to go as someone from the Bible, so she was turning Grace into John the Baptist with his head on a platter.

"There's no such thing as demons," Prudence said, only because she hadn't been the one to hear the story first. She hacked at the sheet with scissors, the blades dull as butter knives. When she managed a hole, she threw the sheet over Grace's head.

Ryan Kitter's whole family were missionaries. They had returned from Africa ahead of schedule, due to the demon, and were camping in the church basement until they found a house. They got to cook on hot plates and take sponge baths. Prudence thought that if anyone deserved to camp in the church basement, it was her own family, since her father was the one who might be the minister. He'd been ordained in three states. At the Moberlys' house, the girls were stuck in a dark, damp room that smelled like motor oil. Before the Moberlys had done it over for their daughter, who was grown, it had been a garage, and twice already Prudence had seen centipedes, one rippling into a crack between cement blocks, one behind the framed picture of Jesus over the bed.

"Ryan likes to be in a dark room," Grace said, pushing her head through the hole in the sheet. "And he doesn't talk to anyone except his mother."

"Well, maybe he doesn't have anything to say," said Prudence, regarding her with a frown. Grace still looked like herself, only in a brown sheet now, blond hair coming out of her braid, and nothing like John the Baptist.

In the picture over the bed, Jesus wore a robe with billowing sleeves and a rope belt, and Prudence needed something to tie around Grace's waist. She rummaged through the cardboard box of odds and ends that Mrs. Moberly had provided. At home in North Carolina, their mother kept old towels and drapes in a trunk, and a drapery cord would have done the trick. But at home they would not be dressing like Bible characters for a party; instead they would have already gone trick-or-treating the night before. They would have worn last year's outfits switched around—Prudence as a floor lamp, Grace as a blue crayon—since their mother wasn't in any kind of shape to make new ones. Here in East Winder, Kentucky, no one was of a mind to trick-or-treat, because Halloween was pagan.

"Ryan's father thinks he has a demon and his mother isn't sure," Grace said. "They took him to doctors, but a doctor can't do anything against a demon. Anna saw a man with a demon swallow a sword in Tennessee. She saw another demon bend a man in half when her dad tried to cast it out."

Prudence made it a point not to be interested. She said, "Really?" and "Hmmm," as she unearthed a scarf and tied it around Grace's waist, so that the ends hung down, then pulled and tucked at the sheet. She put her hands on her hips and stepped back to look. "Not bad," she said. "We'll draw you a beard with eye pencil, but you've got to have a knife or a hatchet or something to make it look real. And a platter."

Mrs. Moberly stood barefoot on the linoleum in front of the kitchen sink, peeling apples for a pie. Her feet were puffy, and it looked like she'd picked her baby toenails clean away. Prudence's mother, who was still sleeping upstairs in the Moberlys' bedroom, had always told Prudence to keep her shoes on; if anyone wanted to see her bare feet, they would ask.

"How're the costumes coming?" asked Mrs. Moberly through a mouthful of apple peel. She wore a blue-and-white-checked apron and had made covers of the same material for the toaster, coffeemaker, and some other small appliance that Prudence couldn't make out by its shape.

"Fine," Prudence said. "Could we please borrow a meat cleaver?"

"A meat cleaver?" Mrs. Moberly's hands stopped, knife poised over a peeled, cored apple. It looked naked and cold. "What Biblical character used a meat cleaver?"

"It's a secret," Prudence said, before Grace could open her mouth.

"A meat cleaver in church? I don't think so," said Mrs. Moberly. "Someone could get hurt. How about another idea? How about you go as a shepherd? Mr. Moberly has an old cane somewhere. Or Mary? Mary never used a meat cleaver."

"No one's *using* it," Prudence said.

"Meat cleavers are sharp," said Mrs. Moberly. "Meat cleavers are not toys. I don't think your mother would be happy if I allowed you to go to church with a meat cleaver. She's not feeling very well as it is." Mrs. Moberly sliced the apple into eighths in four deft strokes. "Your father tells me she likes apple pie."

"She's feeling fine," Prudence said. "She's just tired."

Mrs. Moberly looked at Prudence and smiled in the way adults sometimes smiled at Prudence, lips peeling back from patiently clenched teeth. Then Mrs. Moberly smiled at Grace, who looked at her feet. "What's that you're wearing, Grace?" Mrs. Moberly said. "Let me guess. You're Mary Magdalene, or Ruth."

Grace shook her head.

"Esther?"

"A man," Grace said.

"Moses?"

"It's a surprise," Prudence said again. "How about some tinfoil? We could save it and you could use it again to cover something."

"Tinfoil I can do," said Mrs. Moberly, and handed her the box. "Listen, girls," she said, smiling again. "What do you think of your visit so far? Think you might like to live here?"

"We won't live *here*," Prudence said. "We'll have a parsonage like at home."

"Well, yes," said Mrs. Moberly. "That's what I meant. East Winder's quite a town. I think living here would do your mother a world of good."

Prudence stared at Mrs. Moberly and raised her left eyebrow, something she'd taught herself how to do. Mrs. Moberly's eyes did not seem to be any real color. Under one eye, Prudence could see a tiny length of blue vein beneath Mrs. Moberly's skin, like a fading pen mark.

Mrs. Moberly blinked at her once and turned to Grace. "How about you, dear? Wouldn't you like to live here?"

Prudence answered for Grace as she pulled her toward the kitchen door. "We don't care," she said in her boredest voice.

I don't care was what their mother had to say about moving. Her name was Joyce, and *I don't care* was what she said about many things, usually at the end of a long, tired sigh. Then she'd talk on the phone to her sister, Char—who wasn't saved—and go to bed in the middle of the day, sometimes for days in a row, and when Prudence went in to kiss her good night, she'd already be asleep and smelling like damp books. Yancey said it had to do with the baby who died before he was born in August, but when Aunt Char came to stay for a week she said no. She said this was Joyce in college all over again, or just Joyce waking up, finally, and coming apart, which he should have expected. Yancey said what's that supposed to mean, and Aunt Char said it means nothing, nothing at all, and that Joyce had made her bed. (Joyce used to testify, proudly, that her family in Greenville thought she was crazy for loving the Lord.

She'd been raised twice-a-year churchgoing Methodist, not evangelical. Yancey's preaching had been what saved her before they got married, and Prudence could tell that Aunt Char didn't like that fact one bit.)

Back in the spare room Prudence emptied out the cardboard box of odds and ends. She cut the box apart at the folds, traced the top of Grace's head in the center of one of the long sides, cut out the circle and finally taped on sheets of tinfoil. Then she fitted the whole platter over Grace's head and bunched part of the sheet into the hole at her neck to hold it steady.

Grace squinted at herself in the mirror.

"Do your head this way," Prudence said, leaning her head to the side and fluttering her eyelids. "Try to look like you just got your head cut off."

Grace stuck out her tongue and said, *"Blllhh."* Her head lolled to the side. Then she shrugged her head out of the platter and began cutting out a long, curved knife shape Prudence had drawn on another piece of cardboard. "They tried sending Ryan Kitter to regular school last week," Grace said. "He went to first grade with Anna King."

"Hmmm," said Prudence. She peered into the Moberlys' closet, where she'd already found her own costume. Behind the coats and jackets and Mr. Moberly's old suits hung several leotards clipped to hangers with clothespins, and one pink tutu, the tulle gone flat and limp as a newspaper, all from when their daughter had taken ballet. Inside a box underneath the pink tutu, Prudence had found a spangly halter top with matching tights and a long, gauzy skirt, store tags still attached.

Now Prudence took out the costume and laid it on the bed. The halter was red with long sleeves and tiny round mirrors sewn on and yellow embroidery everywhere. The neck and sleeves had silky yellow fringe, and at the bottom edge, just above where her belly button would show, the fringe ended in tiny wooden beads that clacked softly against each other.

"In the lunchroom he stood at the trash can and ate all the bread pudding and creamed spinach that nobody wanted, and when the teacher caught him and made him stop, he cried. Then he threw up, then he threw a fit, and then they took him right out of school." Grace stopped cutting, her scissors wedged deep in the cardboard, and eyed the costume. "Ooooh. Who are you again?"

"Salome," Prudence said. "The one who asked for your head on a platter."

Prudence slipped off her pants and pulled on the tights and skirt. She did a practice kick out to the side, and the gauzy material traveled up into the air with her leg then floated down. It was see-through. In the picture Prudence had seen in a book in her father's study, Salome was a dark-skinned, smiling, barefoot girl with her hair pulled back, wearing an outfit a lot like this one. Her arms had been raised high above her head, her body in mid-sway, a gentle version of the bump-and-grind Prudence had perfected from a dance show on television, before her father found out she was watching.

No wonder the king had wanted to give Salome anything she wanted. Prudence had curly dark hair, too—almost black—and now she pulled it into a ponytail so tight it made her eyes slanty. She moved her hips in a little circle and waved her arms, first out in front of her, then to her sides, then over her head.

"Does Mrs. Moberly know you're wearing that?" Grace said.

"Mrs. Moberly is a pain."

"I want to be someone who dances."

"You can't dance if your head's cut off."

"*You're* not even supposed to dance," said Grace, and it was true, though the Reverend Yancey Boyd said it wasn't because of dancing itself, but what dancing led to.

"This is different," said Prudence. "It's pretend."

Grace crimped tinfoil onto the blade of the cardboard knife and began coloring the handle black with a Magic Marker. "Once a demon gets in, you act different," she said. "They get in when you get cut open and bleed. Anna's not allowed to have her ears pierced. In Africa, Ryan was crossing the street with their house woman and they got hit by heathens in a truck. They were holding hands and she died and he broke his arm. The bone was sticking out through his skin, and that's when it happened. Demons sneak in wherever they can, and someone has to get them out so you can go back to the way you were. Tonight Anna's dad is going to get the demon out of Ryan. It's a secret, because it's not that kind of church, but Anna's dad says it should be."

Prudence had the halter on over her shirt, and she was stuffing the bosom with Grace's dirty undershirt from the day before. "Stop talking about that," she said. "At the party they'll have to guess who we are, so I'll go first and do my dance, then I'll stop and say, 'Cut off the head of John the Baptist, voice crying in the wilderness, who eats locusts and honey, and give it to me on a silver platter.' Then you come on up and stand beside me."

"What do I say?"

"You don't say anything. We'll have the knife on the platter and ketchup for blood and you just walk like this," Prudence staggered around the bed. "You could collapse, maybe, or just follow me away. Wait and see. Everyone else will be Mary and Joseph and Noah or some other dumb thing."

"A demon could have gotten into Mom when the baby came out," Grace said.

Prudence stopped staggering. "No," she said. "She is just very tired. She just needs her rest." Prudence kept looking at Grace until Grace nodded. Then Prudence pulled up her shirt to see what the halter would look like against her stomach.

"Ryan has a demon of shock," Grace said.

Prudence sucked in her stomach until it looked hollow. Sexy. She turned her back to the mirror and looked over her shoulder for the rear view.

"Mom could have a demon of tiredness," Grace said.

Prudence kept sucking in her stomach until it hurt.

"Don't say that anymore," she said, gritting her teeth. "That's the stupidest thing I've ever heard."

THE REVEREND Yancey Boyd had eyes so light they almost weren't blue at all, and wavy hair close to his head, and when he talked he sounded wise. Aunt Char said that Joyce married him because he looked like Paul Newman, and because he was sincere, though she said it was no excuse. Prudence was used to women going weepy around him, so it was no surprise when at dinner Mrs. Moberly started sharing the heartache of their daughter.

Belinda Moberly had grown up and gone to college, began Mr. Moberly (a good, evangelical college, put in Mrs. Moberly), and under the influence of a philosophy professor, said Mr. Moberly (who was later fired, said Mrs. Moberly), she'd first become a Unitarian, and then an atheist. And she was living in sin, out of wedlock, with a firefighter.

"We did our best," said Mrs. Moberly. "I don't know what else we could have done."

Over the table hung a low, stained-glass chandelier that Mrs. Moberly had made in a class, which cast a ring of tiny yellow crosses around the walls of the wood-paneled dining room.

"She has a good foundation," the Reverend Yancey Boyd said to Mrs. Moberly, and he patted her hand. The patting of hands was usually Joyce's department. She took care of the comforting while Yancey did the talking. It wasn't a good idea for him to touch too many women. He was that handsome. "When children have been brought up in the Lord, He marks them for life. Children"—Yancey passed a hand over Grace's blond head—"have their own kind of openness to the Lord. They may grow up and try other roads, but something inside them always knows better. I believe your daughter has a great advantage."

The Reverend Yancey Boyd sounded encouraging, but he looked sad. Before supper Prudence had found him sitting on the bed beside Joyce, trying to make her eat some crackers from the tray Mrs. Moberly had fixed. Prudence couldn't see her mother's face, but she could hear her whispering how she shouldn't have tried to come, and Prudence had seen how the curl she'd put in her hair the day before, for the trip, had flattened out against her head.

"I don't understand it," Mr. Moberly was saying about his daughter. He was a plumber with shoulders so wide that Prudence didn't see how he could crawl under any sink. He split a biscuit in half and buttered it, and when he finished he put the whole bottom of the biscuit into his mouth.

"I tell her we want her to be happy," Mrs. Moberly said, "and she tells me happiness is overrated. She says she's as happy as she can be and live with herself. I ask her, but do you know Jesus as a *personal savior,* Belinda, that's real happiness—you know, Reverend—and she tells me she would believe if she could, but she can't. I don't know what to do with her." When Mrs. Moberly paused to drink her water, her hand shook a little. "I guess we're not promised we'll always understand, are we, Reverend?"

The Reverend Yancey Boyd smiled in a way that made him look even sadder. "No," he said, "we are not."

Grace picked at her food. She had the nervous hiccups, which didn't sound like regular hiccups at all, but like breathing with little coughs. And she was chewing at the inside of her mouth, which she wasn't supposed to do. Once she'd made herself bleed. Prudence nudged Grace with her elbow, and Grace stopped.

BY THE TIME THEY reached the church parking lot that evening, it was dark and cold. The leaves smelled like fall turning into winter. Prudence had stuffed the platter down the front of Grace's long pink parka like a shield, to hide it, and she'd hidden eye pencil and lipstick and ketchup packets from Burger King in the pockets of her own coat. She'd put pants on over her tights and rolled up the gauzy skirt, too, because she thought Mrs. Moberly might recognize it before their turn.

"Where are the Kitters staying?" Prudence asked, as they walked through the parking lot toward the back entrance.

"Who?" asked Mrs. Moberly.

"The boy with the demon," said Grace, stomping up the cement steps to the door.

"What?" Mrs. Moberly said. She shifted a Tupperware container of cookies to her other hand and held open the church door. Inside, she squatted down beside Grace and peered into her face. "What demon?"

"Never mind," Prudence said. "What do the Kitters

sleep on? Do they have a bed or just nap mats? Do they have a sofa and chair and television or just Sunday-school furniture?"

"I wouldn't know," Mrs. Moberly said. "I haven't seen it. It's their home, you know, for now, until they find a house. You can't just go charging into people's homes unannounced, even if they do live in the church."

"I wouldn't go charging in," Prudence said.

"You're going to have a great time at the party," said Mrs. Moberly, steering them down the basement steps. "Just think of all the new friends you'll make here." Mrs. Moberly spoke in a bright voice and smiled so forcefully her jaw muscles bulged.

They moved down a wide, dim hall toward the bright doorway of the fellowship room at the far end. Three narrow halls branched off on either side of this wide hall, and at these dark openings the air came cool and quiet. Prudence lagged behind and slipped down the last hall before the fellowship room. She tried two doors, but they were locked. She peered through the long, narrow windows over the doorknobs, but it was too dark to see anything.

Mrs. Moberly appeared silhouetted at the mouth of the hall. "Did we lose you?"

"No," said Prudence.

The fellowship room was full of kids and parents. A girl wearing a dingy white sheep hood with ears, her straight hair sticking stiffly out around her face, came right up to Grace and hugged her.

"Hi, Anna," Grace said. Prudence disliked hugging. She

ignored Anna and checked the back of the room where tables had been set up with punch and treats, and the front of the room where kids were jumping off a foot-high wooden collapsible stage.

Mrs. Moberly hovered. "Why don't you take off your coat now," she said to Prudence. "It's warm in here, and look, Anna's in her costume."

"I'm cold," Prudence said. "We both are." She shivered, for good measure, and so did Grace.

Mrs. Moberly smiled the hard smile.

"It's very cold in here," Prudence said. "Someone should probably do something about it."

If the Reverend Yancey Boyd had been there, he would have made her mind Mrs. Moberly, and then he would have marched her back to the house and made her change. He didn't even want her wearing a two-piece bathing suit that showed her belly in the summertime, much less a skimpy dance costume. But tonight he was the guest speaker at a youth lock-in across town, at the high-school gym. Their mother had been the one who'd planned to come to the All Saints' Day party.

"I'd be happy to carry those cookies into the kitchen for you," Prudence said, taking the Tupperware container from Mrs. Moberly.

"Well, sure," said Mrs. Moberly. "But don't go running off. You'll want to meet some girls your age."

In the kitchen across the hall, a tall, thin woman with red hair was slicing through pans of Rice Krispies treats. "Are you Al and Debbie's youngest?" she asked Prudence.

"No," said Prudence. "I'm Yancey and Joyce's oldest."

"Oh, yes," said the woman, "the new pastor's daughter. I'm Mrs. Spode."

"He *might* be the new pastor," Prudence said, but she said it in a nice way.

"He will be if my husband and I have anything to say about it," said Mrs. Spode. She lifted out sticky squares with a spatula and stacked them on a plate. "This church needs someone to get it back on track. People get some strange ideas."

"What ideas?" Prudence asked.

"Oh, nothing for you to worry about," said Mrs. Spode. "Is there a costume somewhere under that pretty coat?"

"Yes," Prudence said, but just then a small Mary entered, holding a blue hand towel that was a Mary-headpiece for Mrs. Spode to pin back on. Then another woman led more children into the kitchen because it was almost time to line them up for the costume show. There were two Marys, a Joseph, a Moses with swimming-pool kickboards for tablets, a donkey, a sheep, a shepherd, a Noah, and a King David with a paper crown. Mostly they looked like children wearing pajamas.

Prudence found Grace and herded her into the corner. She unzipped Grace's coat and extracted the foil-covered platter. With eye pencil she sketched on a mustache and was working on the beard when she felt a poke at her shoulder.

"Well, now," said Mrs. Spode. She reached down and touched the platter. "What's the story, here?"

"I'm doing her beard," Prudence said. "She's John the Baptist."

"Oh, terrific," said Mrs. Spode, clapping once. "We don't have a John the Baptist yet."

Prudence smudged the pencil marks into Grace's skin with her fingertips. Grace said, "That's my platter," trying not to move her lips.

Mrs. Spode picked up the platter and carefully turned it over in her hands. "I see. It does look like a platter. Your head goes into this hole, right here?"

Prudence took the platter from Mrs. Spode, who was frowning, and fitted it over Grace's head, securing it by tucking in the sheet. Prudence withdrew the curved cardboard knife from her coat pocket and wedged it tightly into the space between the platter and Grace's neck, at an angle so that it looked stabbing. She was just tearing open a ketchup packet when Mrs. Spode said, "Hold on a sec."

The other children had begun to gather around Grace. "Who is she?" asked Anna King.

Grace jerked her head to the side and showed them the whites of her eyes. She staggered a few steps the way Prudence had shown her.

"Listen here," said Mrs. Spode. "This is very clever—"

"Thank you," said Prudence.

"—but maybe we could do without the blood and the platter and the knife."

"It's not real blood," Prudence said. She turned around to the children who were watching them. "It's not real," she explained. "It's pretend."

"Maybe I'd better see your costume, too," said Mrs. Spode.

"I'm not ready yet," Prudence said. "I have to do my hair. I have to put on my earrings."

"Now is a very good time," said Mrs. Spode.

"Not yet." Prudence raised her left eyebrow, but Mrs. Spode only raised her own eyebrows and said, "Go ahead and take off your coat, please, miss."

Prudence slowly unzipped her coat. She kept it closed until Mrs. Spode took it off her shoulders for her. When Prudence looked down she couldn't see past the halter bosom to her feet.

Mrs. Spode was silent, regarding her. She sucked her lips in against her teeth thoughtfully. Behind Mrs. Spode, the children stared.

Prudence unrolled the waistband of the gauzy skirt until the hem reached her ankles.

"You must be what's-her-name," Mrs. Spode said. She closed her eyes, then opened them.

"Salome," Prudence said. Even though her coat was off and her stomach was bare, she was growing hot. She thought about taking off her pants under the skirt, and decided against it.

"Well," said Mrs. Spode. She seemed about to say more, but instead she turned to the other children and led them out of the kitchen and into the fellowship room, where the parents had set up folding chairs. She told the Biblical characters to go to the stage one at a time and let people guess, then she returned to the kitchen. She shut the door behind her, but Prudence could still make out the first clapping and laughing.

"Listen," Mrs. Spode said, squatting down. "These costumes are very creative."

"I know," Prudence said.

"The problem," Mrs. Spode said, "is that some people might get the wrong idea."

"It's in the Bible," Prudence said. "Everyone knows how John the Baptist died."

Mrs. Spode twisted her mouth at Prudence as though she was sorry she had to do what she had to do. "Not everyone will appreciate the details before them. You've just got to trust me on this one."

"It's not fair," Prudence said.

Against the wall, Grace was chewing the inside of her cheek.

Prudence remembered what she'd heard Aunt Char saying to her mother. "Don't you ever just want to cut loose?" she said to Mrs. Spode. "Don't you ever just want to live a little?"

"Oh, baby, you're something else," said Mrs. Spode. "You've got a row to hoe, I tell you." She pressed her hand to her forehead. "Listen. How about I go get you a couple choir robes. They're gold and heavy, and you can be two angels."

"I don't want to be an angel," Grace said. She had a packet of ketchup between her teeth, trying to open it.

Prudence heard Mrs. Moberly before she saw her. She entered the kitchen with a quick, sharp breath that had some voice in it. "Where did you find that?" Mrs. Moberly said, staring at Prudence's chest, then at the long skirt.

"You said we could use anything," Prudence said. "You said, 'Help yourself.'"

Mrs. Moberly shook her head. "Belinda never wore that. We put our foot down on that one."

"We're Biblical characters," Prudence said. "You said to come as a Biblical character."

"I had a bad feeling about this." Mrs. Moberly turned to Mrs. Spode. "I knew I should have checked to see what they came up with. Reverend Boyd's preoccupied with his wife sick."

"She's not sick," Prudence said.

Mrs. Moberly opened her mouth, then looked at Mrs. Spode, then closed it again.

"She's not," Prudence said to Mrs. Spode. "She's very tired and needs her rest."

"She's got a little bug," Mrs. Moberly explained.

"Well, there's something going around," Mrs. Spode said.

"She's not sick," Prudence said again. "She's not sick, she's not sick." She heard herself speaking over and over, but she couldn't stop, and she couldn't seem to say anything else. She clamped her mouth tightly closed, because she thought her voice might be starting to sound like tears.

Mrs. Spode squeezed Prudence's shoulder. "Look, Mary Anne, I was telling Prudence here that they could put on choir robes—you know those pretty gold ones?—and go as angels. We could even tape on some paper wings, or make halos or something."

"I think it's a little late to construct anything fancy," Mrs. Moberly said.

Grace's ketchup packet came open and she held it between her teeth, squeezing with her lips so that the ketchup dribbled down her chin and collected in a soft gob on the platter in front of her face. From there it began a slow red slide toward the edge.

Mrs. Spode opened the kitchen door to check on the show. The children were restless. Noah kicked the donkey, and one of the Marys had stuck the head of a baby Jesus under her robe to nurse. "Looks like I'm needed in there," she said to Mrs. Moberly. "Those gold robes are in the closet of the upstairs practice room."

When Mrs. Spode had gone, Mrs. Moberly turned to Prudence and didn't even try to smile. "You two shed these getups right now, and then you stay put and be ready when I come back, hear? I don't want to have to tell your parents you didn't get to be in the show. I don't want to have to explain why."

Prudence kept her mouth tightly closed. She stared into the air just over Mrs. Moberly's head, and soon Mrs. Moberly was gone. As her footsteps faded up the back stairs off the kitchen, Prudence and Grace were sneaking past the fellowship room, headed down the hall the way they'd come in.

Prudence quickly turned off the wide main hall straight into one of the narrow dark halls of Sunday-school rooms.

They made two more turns until it was so dark that Prudence couldn't even see her hand in front of her. The basement went on and on. She remembered a story she heard once, about a maze so confusing that once inside you could turn down every single path you could find and never get it right. You could just keep trying out different turns until you died of hunger, or until whatever kind of animal or monster it was they'd put in the maze to go after you got to you.

The wooden beads on her halter made their small noises against each other, and Prudence wrapped her arms around her middle to still them. She was having a hard time breathing in her regular way.

"Prudence," Grace whispered. "Where are you?" Grace's platter bumped against the wall with a dull scraping.

"Here." Prudence stopped and Grace ran into her; Prudence felt ketchup, wet and sticky on her bare back.

Then Prudence could see her hand again, just barely, because down one of the hallways a light glowed through the long window above a doorknob. Prudence moved toward the light.

"I hear singing," Grace said.

"Shhhh," said Prudence, but she could hear it, too. It sounded like five or six people, and Prudence crept toward the door and peered through the bottom of the narrow window.

A small, thin boy with curly brown hair and an arm in a cast sat in a Sunday-school chair, his eyes closed. Two men and one woman had their hands on the boy's neck and head. The woman was crying and trying to sing at the same time. They were singing that song about the lovely feet of the mountains that bring good news, which had never made any real sense to Prudence. On the floor were two mattresses made up with sheets and blankets.

"Let *me* see," Grace said, but Prudence ignored her. She pressed her forehead against the glass.

"It's no big deal," she whispered after a time. "It's just people standing around a boy. They're laying hands." She knew all about laying hands—sometimes her parents touched people while praying for them so the Holy Spirit could move.

Another man and woman had placed their hands on the backs of the people touching the boy's neck. They all closed their eyes and sang the first verse of "Holy, Holy, Holy," swaying to the words. The man standing behind the boy began speaking over the singing, but it was hard to make out the words through the door. The boy had opened his eyes and was blinking quickly. The fingers of his good arm fretted at the soft, worn edge of his cast.

"Who are you?" the man said now, loud and deep, clear enough for Prudence to hear. She could feel his voice on the door.

"Help him, Lord," said another man.

"Yes, Lord," said a woman.

The first man gripped the boy's shoulder. "Who are you?" he asked again, and the boy moved his mouth, but Prudence couldn't hear.

"That's Anna's dad talking," Grace whispered, wedging her face beside Prudence's.

"No," said the man. The singing was over and his voice was clear as day. "No. I am not speaking to Ryan, but to the evil within."

Prudence thought the group looked too ordinary to be casting out a demon. The men were in plain old slacks and jeans, and one of the women wore sneakers with her skirt. Under the fluorescent lights, their faces loomed pale and big. Even with their eyes closed, they squinted, like they were all trying very hard to remember something.

"It's no big deal," Prudence said again, but she couldn't stop watching.

Anna's dad looked up to the ceiling and started to pray. He said how Ryan was not in control of his body. He said the forces of darkness had taken advantage of this little boy's weakness, and an evil spirit had manifested itself in Ryan's behavior. He said it was a cowardly thing to use a little boy, but that was the kind of method Satan stooped to. He might look like this little boy and sound like this little boy, but indeed he was something very different, something that really wanted only to destroy Ryan. *Impostor,* Anna's dad said, and Prudence felt the word in her stomach.

Prudence pushed Grace away and covered the whole bottom of the window with her face and arms, filling up the glass so her sister couldn't see. She didn't know what was going to happen, and Grace sometimes scared easily.

One of the men began to raise his hand over his head, the movement so slow that the hand looked as if it were floating. He turned his face to the ceiling. "Ruler of all," he said when Anna's dad paused. "You triumph over evil."

Ryan began shaking all over. The woman in sneakers opened her eyes.

"The New Testament tells us we have been given the power," Anna's dad began again, and Ryan started to cry. He scrunched his face up tiny, whimpering. With his free arm he brought his hand to his shoulder and tried to pick off the fingers that clutched him.

"Please," said the woman in sneakers. "He's upset." She moved her thumb back and forth in the boy's hair.

"It's not him," Anna's dad said. From above and behind Ryan, he placed his palms on the boy's cheek. Ryan jerked his head from side to side, but the hands were firm. "What's being upset are the forces of darkness. Just hold him steady."

The woman in sneakers sniffled and shook her head. Prudence kept her eyes on Ryan Kitter.

"In the name of Jesus Christ," said Anna's dad, "I command you to exit this earthly vessel." The sound of his voice resounded off the cement-block walls even after he closed his mouth.

Prudence held her breath, watching for something to leave Ryan's body. He went so still she thought maybe he'd fainted. Anna's dad loosened his grip on the boy's face. Suddenly Ryan lurched to his feet, yanking his shoulders back and forth to shake off the hands and upending his chair, which skidded across the room on its side. The woman in sneakers cried out, "Ryan!" and a man said, "Oh," in a soft, surprised way, but nobody moved. They seemed frozen, their hands still outstretched, now hovering over nothing, while the boy made for the door.

Prudence grabbed Grace and pulled her into the back hall and around a corner. The first room they came to was locked, but the door to the second one opened, and they crouched just inside, listening hard. A moment later Ryan pushed through and slammed the door shut, darting into the far corner of the room. The windows near the ceiling gave off a faint glow from the lights of the parking lot, and Prudence could just make out his dark shape against the wall. She listened to him breathing heavy through his nose, and when she heard more footsteps in the hall, she reached up and locked the door.

Then the boy was crying again, moaning softly.

Grace leaned in close to Prudence and clutched her arm as Prudence rose and made her way across the room through the dark, past tables and chairs and an upright piano. She reached out and touched the boy's head, and he scooted away. It sounded like he was saying "Oh no, oh no, oh no," over and over. Prudence had heard plenty of kids cry, but this seemed older, like the time she'd been dropped home early from school and found her mother sitting with her forehead on the kitchen table, sobbing, her arms dangling down by her chair like they'd come out of their sockets.

"Don't be scared," Prudence said. "It's just me and my sister."

Someone jiggled the doorknob, then knocked on the narrow glass window. Prudence didn't turn around. A woman called Ryan's name, her voice muffled.

Ryan kept crying. Prudence's eyes adjusted, and she could see him huddled against the wall, hunched in on himself.

"Don't cry," Prudence said. "You shouldn't cry like that. You'll cry your eyes out." She was watching him very carefully. If there was such a thing as demons, and they looked and sounded just like people, she wondered how you were supposed to know when one was gone.

"Ryan?" called the woman at the door. Then her footsteps hurried away.

"Do you have a demon?" Grace asked. Her tinfoil platter glinted in the streetlight. The edge of it had bent over her shoulder on one side, and her face and neck were smeared with ketchup. The knife jutted out from her neck at a forty-five-degree angle.

Ryan looked up at her and sucked in a great, moaning sob.

Prudence knelt down beside him. "It's ketchup," she said. Then she thought that maybe they didn't have ketchup in Africa. "She's just dressed up," Prudence said. "She's John the Baptist." She told him all about John the Baptist and Salome, how the king liked Salome's dance so much that he promised her anything, and how Salome's mother, a spurned woman, had told her just what to ask for. When Prudence finished, she rose and stood in the light from the high window so the boy could see. He'd grown quieter, but when she stopped talking, he started to cry again.

"Hey," Prudence said. "You just watch me. I didn't get to do my dance before. When Salome dances she gets whatever she wants, and I want you to stop crying." Prudence began humming a little tune. She started with just her hands and let the movement travel up her arms and into her shoulders, then down her whole body. The wooden beads slapped her stomach.

Ryan's mouth was open. He looked like a sad boy, sad in a part of him no one could touch. Prudence was thinking that it would be better if there *was* a demon than if there wasn't. That way something would be in him and then it would be gone, and he would be all right. She danced in and out of the light, and Ryan's crying grew softer. She hummed a little louder and danced some more, and soon she didn't hear him crying at all.

"It's working," Grace whispered.

There were footsteps again in the hall, and the faint jingle of keys. In a moment or two the lights would come on and Prudence knew she would be in big trouble. They would be taken back to the Moberlys', where she would most likely be disciplined, and where her mother lay in the upstairs bedroom, her face to the wall, and there wasn't anything Prudence could do about it. But as Prudence did a little boogie with her hips, she thought she heard Ryan giggle. Aunt Char had shown her some old-timey dances, and she did what she could remember of the twist, then she started in on the chicken, Ryan and Grace now laughing, laughing hard, gulping in air, their voices high and silly, and when the door opened and the lights came on Prudence closed her eyes and kept on dancing.

The Bell Ringer

ARLY DECEMBER, outside a department store, the coldest Minnesota winter in ten years. Because Esther's wrists hurt and she is rigid with cold, she has taken to holding the handle of the bell between two gloved fingers and, not moving her hand at all, jiggling her whole body up and down like a kid who has to pee. From nine in the morning to nine at night this spasmodic dancing, the reflection in the plate-glass window something she tries to avoid: her small frame huge and stiff in layered clothes, borrowed blue parka with the hood zipped into a tube in front of her face, and a bright red apron that reads "I am a bell ringer" in white block letters, as if anyone could doubt it. The aprons were distributed just two days ago. They distinguish bona fide bell ringers from the rash of false, apronless bell ringers with stolen kettles, a trend in the Northeast that seems to be headed Esther's way.

The bell's the thing, a collection technique like no other, and the organization has patrols to make sure it's always ringing. Esther knows of one boy, stationed at a department store across town, who rang only when people approached. Someone drove by and made note, some officer he didn't recognize. A report was made; he was warned. It's serious stuff, this army that is not the real army but damn close in single-mindedness.

Real army—military—veterans sometimes shuffle to Esther's kettle and empty their pockets, peeling off gloves with shaky fingers and scooting change toward the hole with horny nails. Because the organization gave out free coffee in WWII and the goddamn Red Cross charged a nickel. Other people search frayed pockets and worn purses, some offering proud, bitten-off phrases about free turkeys and summer camp for their kids that they seem not to want Esther to acknowledge. Once in a while someone exiting the mall will bring her coffee, impressed that she stands in the cold for charity. Esther feels guilty when this happens. She fights herself not to reveal that she isn't even a member, that in fact she is paid for ringing the bell. It's a work-study between the organization and the college where she will start all over again, at twenty-four, in January. She picked Minneapolis because the colder the city, the more you got paid. And because she could stay with her sister.

She would like to be a member, maybe. She needs structure, and the organization has rules and people in charge. Rankings and schools and protocol, uniforms and brass bands. She might even like to be in the timbrels, who twirl and jump in their routines in church on Sunday mornings, their tambourines making a joyful noise.

Above the near-empty mall parking lot, the gray Minneapolis sky seems a solid thing, pressing down into Esther's vision. It's too cold to snow. The cold settles in her shoulders as a visible hump. By ten-thirty at night, when Sergeant Margaret finally drops Esther off at her sister's house where everyone is already in bed, she stands under the hot shower until she turns red as a lobster.

AMY THINKS Aunt Esther smells good, like the stiff black jacket with zippers she showed up in, even though she's been wearing a parka for days. When Aunt Esther talks, she sounds like Amy's mother, because they both come from Kentucky. Aunt Esther laughs at Amy's father and the rest of the people in Minneapolis, who talk through their noses. Her father laughs back when Aunt Esther laughs, but if Amy's mother laughs, too, her father stops laughing and looks at his fingernails.

Aunt Esther sleeps with Amy even though Amy's bed is only a twin. Aunt Esther takes the outer edge, because she gets in late and has to get up early, and Amy sleeps up against the wall, clutching her stuffed white bird and feeling pressed, which she likes. She tells her mother that sleeping next to the wall makes the room taller than usual, the ceiling very far away. Amy is six years old—twenty years younger than her mother, eighteen years younger than her Aunt Esther.

Aunt Esther sleeps wearing a yellow smiley-face T-shirt and black bikini panties. One morning Amy wakes before Aunt Esther and counts eleven purple-and-red lines the length of her little finger, one laid above the next like a train track climbing the white skin up out of the black panties. The lines go up the side of her aunt's bottom to where her waist curves in. After the Salvation Army van leaves, Amy asks her parents about this. Her mother, whose name is Bonnie, says, Lines like wrinkles? Her father, whose name is Hammond, says, Lines like a tattoo? and then explains tattoos. Amy says no, purple red lines, pushed-in lines that don't look like anything but lines, except the ones at the top that are scabs, too. Scratches? Bonnie says. Cuts? says Hamm. Amy shrugs and her mother says she hopes Amy didn't stare, because it isn't polite to stare, and Amy says she didn't stare.

ON BONNIE'S DAY OFF from the jewelry counter at Service Merchandise, she sees Amy to the school bus and then takes a thermos of decaffeinated coffee out to the new room Hamm has been building off the living room. What used to be their sliding glass door to the backyard now slides open to the new room. It's still a shell of plywood and two-by-fours with two windows and a second set of sliding glass doors to the outside, but no insulation or drywall up yet and just planks for a floor. Someday it will be a master bedroom, with room for a boudoir chair in a corner, which Bonnie wants, and a television cabinet at the end of the bed, which Hamm wants but which makes Bonnie think of a hotel room.

For now Bonnie goes to the room to work on projects for the "Art for Life" class she's taking at the Community Center. The room's a cold place to work, but Todd, her instructor, has suggested carving out a private spot at home. Bonnie sits in a lawn chair in the middle of the room. She wears three sweaters and a down vest. She drinks coffee and watches her breath, which makes her want to smoke again, though she won't. They are supposed to be trying for another baby, though lately when Hamm touches her it only tickles, and she fidgets until he gets fed up and quits.

She imagines Esther's purple lines and wonders what her sister has gotten into. Esther has come to them from Florida, where she ended up with two men in an apartment with lots of chrome and white leather, like something out of *Miami Vice*. One of the men was her boyfriend for a few months, at first, but then not anymore, Esther said. But they still let her stay for free, until they stopped letting her, or until she just left. Bonnie has asked, but Esther's not talking.

Esther sent Bonnie a picture from Florida in which she was sprawled like a starfish on a white leather sofa, looking thin in shorts and a bikini top. The picture had been over-exposed, showing Esther's skin as white as the sofa, her hair so black it looked blue.

Bonnie picks up her sketch pad and a pencil from the floor by the chair. She begins a line drawing of two fat rolls of pink insulation, stacked one on top of the other in the corner of the room beside a metal ladder and a worktable. As instructed, she pays close attention to positive and negative space, doesn't lift her pencil from the page, doesn't look down until she's finished. It's supposed to be one continuous line. When she does look, she sees lumpy shapes that resemble nothing, but they are not supposed to worry about that yet. They have been instructed not to think in terms of wrong.

Her sister is the creative one. There was that thing Esther did with eggshells in high school, a mosaic with bits of eggshell tinted with food coloring that made a shattered-looking picture of her face when she finished. And she took an art class her first time in college, before her nerves gave out—before Chicago, and California, and the time when no one knew where she was, and before Florida. Again Bonnie thinks of the purple lines. There are always possibilities, it seems, that she has never even thought to wonder about.

A month ago, in a hotel room, Bonnie and Hamm had watched a porn movie. She'd never seen one before, not a *real* porn movie with the women mostly shaved and everything showing, even on the men. Hamm had been surprised at a strenuous-looking scene with two men and a woman in a meatpacking plant. The woman, who was completely naked and very pale, had been held aloft facing the bloody floor. Her thighs rested on the shoulders of an also-naked black man, and her arms wrapped the hips of a deeply tanned blond man as she sucked him, his jeans around his ankles. "That's a new one," Hamm said, offhand, on his way to the bathroom. Bonnie had covered herself in the polyester bedspread and wondered about his having watched enough porn to know what was new. On the television screen, in a cabinet at the foot of the bed, the woman had seemed stretched thin among the hanging slabs of beef, as if the two men were pulling her apart.

———

AT NIGHT AUNT ESTHER wakes Amy up, whispering. She tells her about tiny islands in Florida connected by bridges that go on forever over the water. Some of the islands have people living on them, and some are mostly marsh and full of bugs. Aunt Esther promises she'll take Amy there, and they can swim and watch birds. When they drive over the bridges, Aunt Esther says, they'll have contests to see who can hold their breath the longest.

Aunt Esther's lips are peeling and she keeps borrowing Amy's cherry Chapstick. One night when the moon is full, Amy and Aunt Esther get up and open the blinds and sit on the floor under the window. Amy imagines they are the only two people on a small island, surrounded by dark water and a night sky that is dark and light at the same time. "Isn't it still?" says Aunt Esther about the moon, which gets brighter the longer Amy looks at it. "Isn't it the stillest thing in the world?"

ACROSS THE MALL parking lot, the men at the auto service center periodically raise and lower the garage doors to their building. They can hear the bell, all right, because this morning one of them came over to Esther and said, snarling, "I hear ringing in my sleep." From over there the sound can't be more than a persistent tinkle, but up close it's hard as a blow, a twelve-hour clanging self-assault in the cold, cold air. It rings in Esther's head all night long. On good days it drives away all thought; everything is simply parking lot and sky and cold and people stopping or not stopping. Sometimes hours pass as if she's in a trance; sometimes the bell conforms meaningless words to its rhythm, often the last thing she heard someone say as they entered the mall—"Buddy is a minor," for example: "Buddy is a *mi*nor, Buddy is a *mi*nor."

Sundays she has off, but she still gets up before everyone in the house and goes to the Corps with Sergeant Margaret. Margaret plays trumpet in the band and wears a navy blue suit with gold buttons and a stiff navy hat. She is chubby and blond and her skin is pink, pink, pink.

Esther has been to church before, but this is rowdier. It's a big room with folding chairs and a band made up of whatever instruments people can play. There are three trumpets, a drummer with a full percussion set, a trombone, a tuba, and a violin. Everyone plays melody on every song, drowning out Esther's voice even when she's shouting the words to "Be Still, My Soul" from the hymnal. It feels good to shout, like she hasn't since grade school. After the music the timbrels come out with their tambourines, and Esther can't stop smiling at grown women who do this without feeling silly. Inside it makes her feel something like relieved. It's the best thing since Florida, where she baked and baked on the sand until she wasn't anything but hot.

"It's joy," Sergeant Margaret says when Esther tries to explain how it feels. "It's feeling God close by. It's how he wants you to feel all the time, but sin sometimes gets in the way." According to Margaret, sin can be things that Esther hasn't thought of as sin—not only lying and stealing and

killing, but ungenerosity and wastefulness, too. Esther wants
to ask Sergeant Margaret how one joins the army, but she
thinks maybe you're not supposed to ask. Maybe you're supposed to be invited.

Sergeant Margaret gives Esther a tiny pocket Gospel,
and Esther tries to read it on her breaks, but she can't focus
on the tiny words.

HAMM'S WORKSITE IS close to the mall, and Bonnie has
asked him to stop by Esther's kettle on his lunch break. He
waits two weeks, to let Bonnie know he'll do it when he's
good and ready.

When he does stop by, Esther is going up and down on
her toes very quickly, like a big shiver, ringing the bell with
her whole body. She is a tiny, wiry woman with dark eyes
in a small, square face—a smaller version of his wife. The
parka around her face is partially unzipped and her mouth
is moving, giving off little gray puffs of air in the cold.

"Aren't you freezing?" he asks.

"Yes," she says. "Did you know that the Indians used to
make their warriors run barefoot through the snow for
two days, so they'd never feel cold again? A man just told
me that."

"What if it backfired? What if they never felt warm
again?"

Esther wipes her nose with the back of her glove. "That
would suck."

They eat lunch in the mall food court. Esther sets the
heavy kettle on the table between them. It's red and shiny

metal like an old-fashioned toy, with a thick wire handle and a small Masterlock threaded through the latch. When she removes her parka hood, her short black hair separates into spikes, flat in some places, while in others springing up from her scalp like a houseplant.

"So," Hamm says, "what do I hear about people stealing kettles?"

Esther looks up quickly, and Hamm remembers he's not supposed to say anything to make her worry. She's a worrier.

"Not that anyone would steal yours."

"We're supposed to watch for vans that pull up to the curb," says Esther. "They've been taking the sign and the stand, too, so they can set up somewhere on their own." She's looking down, speaking fairly calmly, peeling off the top bun of her hamburger.

Hamm has never spent much time with Esther. He met her first at his wedding, when she was sixteen and wore mittens before and after the ceremony because she wouldn't stop picking a scab in her hair that had grown deep enough to be dangerous. Then he saw her three Christmases ago at his mother-in-law's, when his mother-in-law still hosted holidays. That time Esther seemed perfectly normal to him, as she does now.

"Well, it's probably nothing to worry about," Hamm says. "What are the chances?"

"I'm not worried, actually," Esther says, "and you can tell it to Bonnie. But for the record, low probability has never given me any real peace of mind."

Hamm watches the way her small hands scrape the cheese from the burger. In her complete absorption with a task, she is like a cat cleaning its face, or a dog circling before it lies down. When she eats both the burger and the soft hunks of cheese, separately, Hamm smiles.

"What are you looking at?" Esther asks, sounding tough.

"Nothing."

"Your wife's sister, huh?" says Jerome when Hamm returns to the work site whistling. "That's an old story." Jerome sits in a windowsill they've just installed, drinking coffee from a thermos and smoking.

"Hey, now," Hamm says. "That's not how it is."

"Right," says Jerome. "Is she hot?"

"I don't know," Hamm says. "Not exactly. She doesn't really seem like a girl, sometimes."

"A lesbian?"

"I don't think so. More like an animal. Like when you see a cat you think 'cat,' not male or female cat. I don't know."

"I can't see that," Jerome says. "I usually think 'female cat' when I see a cat."

"She's artistic," says Hamm. "She made a whole picture out of eggshells."

"Oh," says Jerome.

SOME DAYS, ringing the bell means that thoughts Esther would rather forget creep into her head and stick. After lunch with Hamm, on her way back to the kettle stand, she notices a learning store called The Expanding Universe.

It reminds her of something she heard in college, how in such a universe everything is always being torn apart, atom from atom. Esther can feel this slow process, an electricity between her fingers, under her arms, at the roots of her hair. Another day, a man with no gloves and no thumb shakes her hand and laughs as she stares at the smooth salmon-colored scar, unable, at first, to figure out what's missing. Once a woman pushes a wheelchair with a man's enormous bearded head, in a stocking cap, positioned above a jacket that wraps what looks like only a canister where his body should be. The man smiles at her in the nicest way, but later Esther can't decide if she saw what she saw.

It's crazymaking, and after such days Esther will go home and wake up Bonnie so they can do "sweep the floor," or "think of the worst," like they did growing up. It clears her head. But she's only had to do that once or twice. She has very few bad days.

BONNIE WEARS Esther's black leather jacket to her class. She has brought three household objects, which Todd calls "found objects," even though Bonnie has always known they were right there in the junk drawer. She ends up trading them, anyway: her small terra-cotta pot, kitchen magnet with a drawn illustration of marjoram, and used-up ink pen in the shape of a rubber trout for an orange ceramic widemouthed frog meant to hold a kitchen sponge or steel wool, a blue plastic tampon case and a ball of rubber bands the size of her fist.

Her classmates are mostly women her age and one thin, white-haired man named Ronald, who compliments everyone. They all finger their objects and wait for instruction from Todd, who makes a list on the board in his fast left-handed printing.

1. Line up your objects according to size and sketch them with charcoal.
2. Stack your objects on top of each other. Stipple.
3. Draw your objects with colored chalk.

And so on. The room is full of windows, and the fluorescent lights blaze against the dark outside. Everyone works silently while Todd circles the room and flips through their sketchbooks, commenting in low tones on the work they have done outside class.

"Tell me about this," Todd says when he gets to Bonnie. He's looking at her picture of a wizard holding a crystal. She'd thought it would be creative, like the figurines in gift shops.

Bonnie looks at the wizard, which is not badly drawn, for her. She worked hard to make twiggy fingers and a gnarled-looking nose.

"Why did you choose it?" Todd asks.

Bonnie thinks about this, and feels dullness coating her brain like milk. She realizes she thinks wizards and crystals are kind of stupid. She hates those figurines. "I have no idea," she says, taking back her sketchbook and closing it. "I'm trying, but I'm not very creative."

"Oh, trying," Todd says. "Trying ruins everything. Forget how to try."

At home she replaces the found objects in the kitchen drawer.

"You did what?" says Hamm, when she tries to explain the class. He is sitting on the couch with Amy, playing a slow game of checkers.

"It's about seeing," Bonnie says. "It's about looking at ordinary things and noticing their color and shape and size, that kind of thing."

"And then what?"

"And then you just notice things more," says Bonnie, "how all kinds of things look, which enriches your life."

Hamm raises his eyebrows.

"King me," Amy says.

Bonnie shows them the drawings from class. The rubber-band ball in the frog's open mouth, the dual cylinders of the tampon case propped up against the curve of the frog's back. Some of the arrangements now seem sexual. Without meeting her eyes, Hamm hands her the sketchbook, keeping it perfectly balanced with one hand as if it's a tray of breakable objects that could be spilled.

"You did a good frog," says Amy.

ESTHER IS NOT exactly pretty, Hamm thinks, sitting across from her again in the food court of the mall. It's crowded for a weekday, people Christmas shopping on their lunch breaks, well-dressed women with shopping bags striding across the shiny floor, mixing in with the daily mall walkers, elderly people in sneakers and sweatpants.

He has asked her how she liked living in Florida, and she is explaining how it was in Florida that she was finally able to go off her medication.

"It was scary shit, anyway," she says. "I took these pills that calmed me down, right? But what they really did was make me stop doing everything. I would just lie down with my eyes open all the time like a zombie. No sleeping, either. And whenever I stood up, I had to figure out how far away my feet were. I mean, I could put my hand down around my hip, and I swear when I looked down, I thought I was about to touch the floor."

"Weird," Hamm says.

"But in Florida I just sat in the sun every day and let the pills wear off," Esther says. "I did a lot of sleeping. I think I just needed to sleep it off."

"I'm not one for a lot of medicine, myself," Hamm says.

Esther's eyes are bright when she talks. Her small, chapped mouth forms words efficiently. Hamm doesn't ask her anything difficult, anything about the men she lived with or the places she's been or if she feels okay now. She doesn't like to talk about it, Bonnie says, and he doesn't want her to freeze up. He doesn't want to wreck the fact that she's telling him as much as she is, which makes him feel selected. She's not exactly pretty, but she has a spark, an energy that, while not quite healthy, is magnetic. When he thinks of touching her, he imagines that she would feel much like Bonnie, only smaller, and that besides this difference there would perhaps be another difference, obvious only to him—her skin, maybe, would be dryer, or warmer, or covered with finer hairs.

When her half-hour break is up, he helps her on with her sweaters, parka, apron, hood. His hands brush and stroke and yank at the sleeves and hems, as if she's a child, to straighten out all the layers. Outside, he ties the apron around her neck. His fingers rest for a moment on her padded shoulders, and then he gives her a fatherly squeeze. But as he squeezes her shoulders he remembers that underneath all the layers and down the back of her pants are the eleven lines, and this causes him to keep squeezing her shoulders until she stiffens. Or does she? Under so many layers it's hard to tell, but, as if to correct himself, he pats her impersonally on the back.

In the rearview mirror of his truck he watches to make sure she starts ringing the bell, and as he leaves the parking lot, she does.

SOMETIMES AT NIGHT, now, Aunt Esther and Amy whisper to each other for a long time. Amy shows Aunt Esther the paper cut on her finger, from a holiday poster she made at school. Aunt Esther tells her that she read about a man who cut himself on paper at work and it made him sick—there are things you can't see covering every piece of paper, covering everything—and his arms and legs lost all their blood and had to be cut off. Amy tells Aunt Esther that Rick Smiley at school wants her to be his girlfriend, and Aunt

Esther warns her not to let him stick his tongue in her mouth, because after that things get hazardous. The night before Amy's checkup at the doctor, Aunt Esther makes her memorize the two questions you should always ask the nurse before you get a shot: Is that a brand-new needle? and Did you check for air bubbles in the syringe? Air bubbles in the syringe can kill you. At the doctor Amy asks the first question, and her mother frowns. But when her mother asks where she heard it, Amy shrugs and won't say.

When Amy begins to have trouble sleeping, Aunt Esther strokes her hair and tells her to imagine herself sweeping a cabin floor, sweeping the dirt into a pile and then right out the door, packing a rolled-up towel into the crack under the door so no dirt can get back in. Aunt Esther says it doesn't always work for her, but that it might work for Amy. You never know.

ONE NIGHT, after Amy is in bed and Bonnie and Hamm are sitting on the couch watching television and not touching, Bonnie asks Hamm how the new room is coming. She asks him cheerfully, as if progress really might have been made, as if she hasn't set foot in the new addition to check the progress in weeks.

Hamm's eyes are gray and unreadable. He looks at her, and the look doesn't give over to anger or laughing.

"I don't get it," Bonnie says.

Lately Hamm has been spending the evenings painting the ducks-of-the-month he receives by mail, each stamped from a new, naked piece of wood and complete with a duck whistle that sounds the decoy's particular quack. On top of the television sit two mallards, the female brown and spotted, the male with an iridescent green head.

"What don't you get?"

"It was going to be finished by spring."

"Roof's on, windows in, snow can't hurt it," Hamm says. "No rush that I can see. We're not going to be needing it anytime soon." He pauses, blinks at her. "Are we? No baby on the way, unless I'm truly ignorant."

He sounds sad, and Bonnie closes her eyes. She reaches across the couch and puts her hand on Hamm's knee. She runs her fingers up the inside of his thigh. She waits for the prickling of her nerves, the sneak of anticipation between her legs, but her mind won't stay put. She is thinking of class, of her new hunger to express something—she doesn't know what, exactly, but she is surprised by the force of it. She thinks, too, of the scene from the porn movie. The men, one golden and the other gleaming black, with the pale woman among the large red carcasses laced with fat. She remembers disgust tinged with arousal and with a suspicion of Hamm's secret habits. Now she wonders if it may have been, in a way, beautiful. This is what she is thinking when Hamm catches her hand with his.

"Do you mean it?" he asks, his voice holding itself.

"I want to," Bonnie says.

"You want to, or you want to mean it?"

"I want to mean it," she whispers.

"Christ."

Bonnie keeps her eyes closed and listens as Hamm

rises, moves to the kitchen. He fills a glass at the tap—a hollow sound—and shushes his arms into coat sleeves.

"Where you going?" she asks quietly, eyes still closed.

"I am going for a drink," he says, opening the door. "I am going for a drink to enrich my life." The cold air reaches Bonnie, not when the door is open, but after he's closed it behind him.

THE SEASON WEARS ON. Weekdays, cold hours pass before the late-afternoon rush, with almost no one entering the mall through Esther's door. When she's alone, she has begun to suspect that someone is watching her, hiding somewhere close by, waiting to sneak behind her, between her back and the plate-glass window. Her parka hood keeps her vision straight on. When she thinks he's behind her, Esther keeps ringing for a while, acting like she doesn't notice. Then she whirls around, but he's slipped away. There is nothing but the plate-glass window and her reflection, and the pyramid display inside of Mug-n-Mini-Warmer sets for keeping coffee hot at work.

Some days, as the cold from the sidewalk creeps up through her feet and calves, she has to keep looking down at her boots on the two carpet remnants the store manager brought her. She has to keep checking, though she knows it's impossible, to make sure her legs haven't been impaled through the heels on icy steel spikes.

And now that Esther's bangs have grown down past her eyebrows, she imagines the ends are tiny razors, and this makes her jerk her head from side to side and blink until she's dizzy. She almost laughs—her bangs are not razors!—but the laughing turns to shivering. She closes her eyes and thinks of the sun, of heat that turned the inside of her head red, that warmed her eyeballs through her eyelids, that reached her scalp with the prickly feeling of a chill without the cold. Then her eyes open and the sky is bright gray and cold and ringing. Razors. These days go on forever.

Before bed, Amy sneaks a cotton ball under her pillow, and after her mother has tucked her in and kissed her good night, she divides the cotton ball in half and sticks a half in each ear, like when she has an earache. When Aunt Esther comes in, Amy does not open her eyes.

"Amy-Amy," Aunt Esther whispers, fingering her hair, but Amy flails her arm, makes a baby noise, and keeps her eyes closed. It is the first time she has pretended with an adult. She is surprised that Aunt Esther believes her, that she turns away and sighs and slips under the covers. But Aunt Esther's breathing never changes to sleep, and Amy has to stay still a long time.

Two weeks before Christmas, Paula, a woman in Bonnie's class, has already finished her final project. She brings in slides of herself with her mother and her daughter, then projects the slides onto paper taped onto the wall. She traces the negative spaces between the figures, and then cuts them out and arranges the shapes on a bigger piece of paper and watercolors them.

The next week Paula reads a poem she wrote about baking bread with her mother and her daughter, shaping the loaves like their negative spaces, then sharing the bread. She calls the poem "Communion."

"Delightful," Todd says.

Bonnie has not begun her final project because she can't think of anything to do. She returns home from class and stomps around the house, peering into each room for ideas.

"I'll be glad when this class is over," Hamm says. "It's supposed to be Art for Life, right? So how about the rest of your life?"

When Esther comes home Bonnie is still up, sitting alone at the kitchen table, tearing images from magazines. Crayons from Amy's jumbo set are scattered across her open sketchbook, and the entire contents of the junk drawer have been dumped onto the linoleum. Bonnie is rubbing out the colored ink of the magazine pages with her gum eraser, then filling the newly whitened spaces with color. She's trying to find a subject, something to say or understand.

"That thing you did with the eggshells that one time," Bonnie says to Esther without looking up. "How'd you think of it?"

"What?" Esther says. She has brought cold air in with her.

"The picture you did, the mosaic. In high school. How did you think of something like that?"

Esther sits down across the table. Bonnie rubs the mouth off an Oil of Olay model. She blackens the spot with a crayon, and it looks exactly like what kids do to makeup displays in drugstores—fake eyebrows, cavities, bloody noses on the pictures.

Now Bonnie hears Esther's breathing coming short and fast, as if she's whispering, *huh, huh*. She looks up and Esther is making a tiny motion with her head, over and over, the tiny jerking to the side of someone who is describing something and trying to shake the memory of it at the same time.

"Esther?"

"Razor blades in my eyes," Esther says.

Bonnie puts down the crayon and looks into her sister's face. "Stop that," she says.

"Say, 'Pull it together,'" Esther says.

"Pull it together," says Bonnie. It's what their mother used to say, standing at the kitchen sink, wooden spoon in hand, after Esther had said, "cereal, toast, cereal, toast, cereal, toast," for fifteen minutes, giggling nervously, unable to stop repeating the words. "Pull it together," their mother had said, every time Esther opened her mouth, in her no-nonsense, of-course-you-can, don't-be-ridiculous voice. It used to work, but now Esther has started humming, the high-pitched way she does when she doesn't want to hear herself.

"Razor blades?"

Esther nods and hums.

"It's your bangs, I guess." Bonnie gets up and fishes a bobby pin from the junk on the floor. She stands over Esther and smoothes her hair straight back from her forehead, clasping it with the pin. "Close your eyes," Bonnie says, her voice low and controlled.

"You're in a one-room cabin. There's one door and one window. Your worries are on the floor, and you have a broom. Sweep, sweep the floor. Are you sweeping?"

Esther nods.

"Sweep the corners, sweep under the window, sweep everywhere until you have a big pile."

Esther's face scrunches, as if she's trying to see the big pile of her thoughts on the cabin floor. She's stopped humming.

"Sweep it out the door," Bonnie says, and waits. "Better?" she asks when Esther opens her eyes.

Esther says yes, but then she squeezes her eyes shut and jerks her head back and forth. She's almost laughing again, but it's not laughing.

"They're right here. They're hanging from somewhere, right here," she says, hitting her eyebrows with the heel of her hand. "I know they're not there. I can see they're not there. Are they? Right here," she says again, grinding at her brow.

Bonnie is standing over her again, saying, "Think of the worst, remember? What's the worst that can happen? Figure out the worst."

Esther opens her eyes and they are wet brown and wild. Her jawbone pulses as she clenches and unclenches her teeth. "The worst is that they could really be there," she says.

"And?"

"And they would cut my eyes."

"And?"

"And I would go blind, and they would keep cutting into my brain behind my eyes."

"Brains are cut into all the time," says Bonnie, "every day. So are eyes. If that happens, they would put tiny stitches in your eyes and you would heal."

"I would lose part of my brain," Esther says.

"You have brain to spare," says Bonnie. "Everyone has extra. People don't use most of the brain they have anyway." She takes a dishcloth from a drawer, runs cold water over it, and folds it into thirds.

Esther closes her eyes again and Bonnie lays the dishcloth across them. She strokes Esther's hair and eventually Esther stops the shivering-laughing and the tiny jerks of her head. Bonnie helps her to Amy's room and, with the dishcloth over her eyes, Esther manages to sleep.

It comes over the radio at the apartment-construction site that thieves have stolen a Salvation Army kettle outside a grocery store not far from the mall. At lunch Hamm heads over to Esther's kettle, pleased to have something to tell her. If she really is worrying again, like Bonnie says, perhaps he will reassure her, even offer to stand beside her at the kettle for the rest of the day. The sky is dark gray with snow coming. Christmas is four days away.

As it turns out, Esther already knows about the theft. The organization has someone driving around to all the kettles, warning them to watch for two men in a red truck or a white van.

So Hamm finds himself saying things like "Well, hey, your last week of ringing," after they've placed their trays across from each other at a table. He hears his voice loud and too bright.

Esther said the little bit about the organization, but nothing after that. She's blinking rapidly. Her hair is pulled tightly back from her forehead with pins and one of Amy's pink barrettes.

Hamm tries to catch her eye, but while she appears to be looking at him, she is really looking somewhere just to the side of him—at his ear, maybe, or his hair.

"I've got Christmas shopping left," he says. "Amy and Bonnie."

Then Esther does look at him, for one second. There are her small, hot eyes.

"What will you get them?"

Hamm sits back, relieved. "Well Amy, Amy's easy," he says. "She likes stuffed animals, paints, Play-Doh, all that. Bonnie takes care of gifts she gets from us and I buy the gifts she gets from Santa. Usually just one or two. It's Bonnie who's hard." There is something bitter in his voice when he says this.

Esther looks to the side and down, as though she is thinking about something else.

"Yeah," says Hamm. Then, "Nothing's easy about Bonnie." He laughs a low laugh, watching Esther closely. "We don't understand each other anymore," he says. He has never talked about Bonnie to her in any serious way.

Esther does not react. She does not raise her eyes to his and exchange with him a look that would acknowledge anything, any line about to be crossed. She does not shut him down, either. She keeps eating fries, as though he's not there.

"Hey, everything okay?" Hamm asks her.

"What?"

"I just wondered if everything was okay. You seem kind of distracted. Are you worried about the thieves?"

"We've covered that," says Esther.

Hamm feels their rapport slipping. He is surprised at how little it takes.

"But, I mean, now that it's happened here," says Hamm, "and so close by."

"What are you, trying to make me worried?" Esther laughs, like shivering, almost snarls. "What did you, come down here just to see if you could freak me out?" There's suddenly something mean and knowing in the way she looks at him. She has spoken through her teeth.

"Hey now," Hamm says. "You know that's not true." He reaches across the table for her shoulder, and she flinches away.

She gives him a wincing smile. "Just a joke," she says. "God."

Hamm means to leave it there. She does not allow him to help her on with her coat. As he follows her back through the department store, she holds her kettle very close and keeps her head down.

He snatches at her elbow and she stops.

"Hey," he says playfully.

She's looking right at him, no smile of any kind.

"What's with you?" he asks. He can't help sounding childish.

Esther turns around and keeps walking.

Outside, she hooks up the kettle and takes her position beside it. She pulls out her bell and starts ringing the hell out of it. Hamm stands in front of her.

"Sorry about that," he says, trying for levity.

"Okay," she says easily, as if she's ready to get on with her day, ready for him to leave.

He can't leave yet. "Look," he says. "I'm not trying to be a jerk." He clamps his hand around the bell and silences it.

Esther lets go the bell and zips the parka close around her face. She seems, to Hamm, to have grown smaller.

"It's just been nice to have you around," he says. "I mean, I just want you to know that Bonnie and I are here for you." He sounds insincere. It's as if his voice has been switched to a different frequency and everything's coming out wrong. "Esther?" He takes a step away from her, then toward her. When he reaches to hug her—he has not re-alized he was going to do this, he is not a hugging man—she starts to shift away, but then seems to give in, and permits him. In his arms she is bulky, stiff, her own arms at her side.

He waits for her to hug back, even if just as a reflex. Isn't that what people do? But she doesn't hug back. Determined, he hugs her so hard he can feel the fragility of her bony body underneath the layers. In his hand, against her back, the bell clapper clinks once, quietly and without resonance. Esther's feet lift off the ground. Hamm says "whoops" and hopes she will laugh, but she doesn't. Frustrated, he hugs her harder, harder, until she makes a small gulping noise. When he releases her, she steps back and gasps. He hands her the bell and she holds it still.

Back in his truck, he reminds himself that he could have crossed a line, but he didn't. He loves Bonnie—they are just having one of those hard times right now—and he loves her sister, too, like family. He wishes Esther had laughed it off, though, like a normal person.

HAMM IS GONE and the sky is dark with snow coming. The bell is going on and on somewhere beside her, like some little bird hopping around her feet. A van pulls up to the curb and little kids spill out. Another van lowers a man in a wheelchair from the passenger seat on a motorized lift. Two vans. Esther thinks, am I worried? And, I'm not worried, but then she's whispering this to herself.

A woman with red hair and a long leather coat approaches the kettle, takes out her checkbook and writes a check for one hundred dollars.

"Cold," the woman says. "Looks like snow."

But Esther is saying, "Am I *wor*ried? I'm not *wor*ried," to herself, under her breath, to the rhythm of the bell. The woman with the red hair shrugs and stuffs the check into the slot. "Merry Christmas, anyway," says the woman.

Esther's feeling the bell, again, moving her wrists, banging it up and down. *Am* I *wor*ried? *I'm* not *wor*ried. Her breath puffs in front of her face. The bell clangs violently. A pregnant woman pauses at the kettle but then changes her mind and hurries into the store.

Later, another woman carrying a baby with a blue pom-pom on top of its hat stops at the kettle and says, "If you'll take him for a sec, I'll get into my bag."

Esther shakes her head, still chanting into the air.

The woman peers at her. "What's that you're saying?"

"*Am* I *wor*ried," Esther says out loud. "*I'm* not *wor*ried." Esther knows she could never, ever hold the baby because of what could happen—not just that babies can be dropped by accident, but worse, that they can be slammed to the ground, their heads splitting like gourds. That until the worst has happened, there is always the awful possibility of it. There is no way to explain this to the woman, who snuggles her baby closer and averts her gaze as she moves past Esther into the store.

And now Esther can't go back to her sister's tonight, or ever again. She has thought the thought that she will have sex with Hamm. Just the thought—in words, not pictures—full of dread and isolated completely from desire. Just the worst she could think of from how he's looked at her, that she would do it even though she doesn't want to do it. She would do it because the only way to get away from being about to do it is to go ahead and get it over with.

It's also why she is not worried about men in a van coming to steal her kettle, because that's not the worst. The worst—and she shakes her head to keep the thought, in words, from entering her mind (*Am* I *wor*ried? *I'm* not *wor*ried!)—is that she will steal the kettle herself. She does not want the kettle, but there it is—the theft of it— in her mind, spelled out in black letters that she tries to see on the floor of the cabin, sweep, sweep the floor, but the cabin has a plank floor with wide gaps and the letters get stuck.

She unhooks the kettle. Inside the department store, she carries it past the perfume and purses, past the pregnant woman trying on scarves, out into the noisy mall with the waterfall. Down the hallway where the restrooms are, everything is quiet and white walls and slick tile. The hallway is hot. It's like being inside a long, hot white pipe, the watery mall noise far behind and small. At the end of the hallway double doors lead to a deserted loading area outside. The right door has been propped open with a brick, because otherwise the hallway might be too hot for breathing. Under her layers, Esther sweats.

Outside there is a Dumpster. Esther sits on the stoop and works the Masterlock of her kettle with a bobby pin. She thinks of Florida, how she could go back because they were nice to her, always apologizing, and what they wanted wasn't really so bad. Tiny cuts she hardly felt, blood kissed and licked off like forgiveness. During the day when they were gone, she could lie on the hot beach while the sun emptied her head.

The lock springs open against her hand, like something living, and she unlatches the kettle. Dirty coins float in a green paper soup, the red-haired woman's yellow-flowered check unfolding itself in the middle. The money stinks of people's hands and pockets and purses, of everything they've fingered and chosen and eaten. Esther wants none of it. But while she can still fasten the kettle, and walk back down the long suffocating hallway and through the department store, and reattach the kettle to the sign as if she'd done nothing, it doesn't count. She would only be about to steal it again.

Her sweating has stopped. She is cool and not cold. She stands and with both hands shakes the contents into the green Dumpster, the bills landing with tiny pats and the coins jingling against each other. The kettle hits the inside of the Dumpster with an injured clunk.

Wastefulness is wrong, she knows, so many people without so much. But as she reenters the hallway and heads toward the mall noise, she is giddy, walking on air because she's done it and can't worry anymore that she will. Though by the time she reaches the mall, she has already begun to sweat again.

Sergeant Margaret brings Aunt Esther home at four-thirty in the afternoon. Amy's sitter lets them in and then calls Bonnie at work. Sergeant Margaret keeps her arm around Aunt Esther, who is shaking and talking very fast, something about sand and a white pipe, but her words run together and no one responds. She reaches out to touch

Amy's hair, but Aunt Esther's eyes don't look right and Amy moves away. Amy puts on her coat and goes out to the new addition to wait for someone who knows something to come home. She doesn't want Aunt Esther looking at her with scary eyes.

Then Amy's mother and a doctor are there, and they untie Aunt Esther's red apron and unzip her parka and pull off her sweaters and hold her down for a shot, while Aunt Esther talks and talks. Then Aunt Esther is lying facedown on Amy's bed with her nose and mouth right on the pillow, not to the side. Amy watches the whole thing because Bonnie forgets to make her wait in the other room. Bonnie's eyebrows move like she will cry, but she doesn't, not even when Sergeant Margaret hugs her and folds the red apron and asks if she can help.

Later, when Amy's father comes home and everyone else leaves, he and Bonnie go into the bedroom with the door closed, then he comes out and takes Amy to McDonald's for a hamburger. The McDonald's is brighter than usual, and people around them are making noise but it all sounds like buzzing. Amy's food feels like food in her mouth, but it doesn't taste like food. Afterwards they drive around and around to look at Christmas lights in the neighborhoods. When Amy closes her eyes, she still sees the Christmas lights, but the colors are different. Her father talks to her and pats her neck, but Amy is looking at the lights inside her eyes.

Back at home Hamm heads out to the new addition to take stock. With the ladder and a nail gun he begins to install the pink ceiling insulation. He works in the light of the living room shining through the sliding glass doors, late into the night, long after Amy has fallen asleep on the couch.

In Amy's bedroom, Esther sleeps. Bonnie has pulled Amy's miniature rocking chair close to the bed and wedged herself into it so tightly that her left leg tingles. She has removed Esther's shoes, socks, and pants and wiped her face with a cool cloth. Now Bonnie sits and rocks, her knees halfway to her chest, listening to the steady punching of the nail gun in the new addition. She picks up her sketchbook and pencil and stares at her sister's sleeping form.

After a time, Bonnie begins to draw. She sketches the general shape first, Esther's head and neck, the dips and hollows of the bedspread. Then the body outline suggested underneath. After shaping the thin back, the gentle roundness below, Bonnie stops and reaches toward the bed, peeling down the covers to see the rest.

Borderland

F YOU HAD TO COMPARE," asked Shiloh's mother, "who would you say has the happier family? The Peels or your father?" It was a Wednesday night, dusting night. Shiloh was wiping down baseboards with an old pair of cotton underpants, and Roxanne was wiping down the venetian blinds with a wet rag, twanging the thin metal.

"I don't know," Shiloh said. The underpants caught on the baseboard where it was pulling away from the wall. "Um, the Peels, I guess."

"That's what I thought," said Roxanne. "And they probably don't have a perfect marriage, either. I never once said my marriage was perfect. And pregnancy is hard on Marge Peel, you can tell. Two miscarriages in two years. But they've had children and they're sticking it out. I always thought I'd have more children."

"We could get a pet," Shiloh said.

"Pets need attention. And space. We're not home during the day. You have to think about what's fair."

"Turtles don't need space," Shiloh said. The Peels had

four miniature sea turtles in a tank. "They just need a little water."

Roxanne raised the blinds five inches and went to work on the windowsill. "Bob Peel ordered those turtles through the mail," she said. "Isn't that something? Now, if I met someone as nice as Bob Peel, mustache aside, I might consider dating again. Your father, he couldn't handle a woman with her own interests." Roxanne's voice sounded like it was winding up into a tirade, and Shiloh kept her head down. When Roxanne lost her cool, she made more cleaning for them to do. Once she'd dumped out the drawers of Shiloh's dresser onto the floor for more careful refolding. "He couldn't handle that I didn't want to spend my weekends dressing up like a Union wife and carting you around to battle sites. I mean, those *people,* Shiloh. He couldn't handle that I might have my own idea of a good time, you know? My music?"

"I know," said Shiloh. Her mother composed lonely songs with her guitar, holding out wavering notes with her voice while her fingers found the next chords. Bob Peel had told her that when he started his own church, he was going to need someone to lead the singing.

"I'm just glad that you have a good, fatherly example, even if it's not your own. That's going to mean a lot to you someday." Roxanne threw down her rag and slipped on a white cotton glove. "Ready for me to check?" she said, and Shiloh nodded. Roxanne ran her finger along the baseboard, and when she lifted her hand, the gloved finger was still clean.

Over Shiloh's bed hung a shelf of miniature horses from her father and stepmother. Her father lived an hour away, on several acres near the Kentucky River. He'd hinted that he had his eye on a real horse for Shiloh's tenth birthday. Not all her own—she would have to share with her stepbrother and stepsister—and not a full-sized horse, and not a young horse, but still. One-third of a small, old horse was better than nothing. There was a very good chance it wouldn't happen, though. Shiloh's father often said things he would like to do as if he were going to do them, and those things ended up not happening, or happening for a time and then petering out. Like how he'd been going to call her every night right after he'd moved out. He had a good month, then he missed some nights, and then he stopped calling altogether.

Still, sometimes Shiloh allowed herself to imagine holding her hand very flat while big horse lips tickled up carrots and sugar cubes from her palm. She imagined riding across a field, wrapping her arms around the horse's neck, a Confederate girl escaping from the Union army that was burning down her family's farm. Like Sherman who burned down everything that got in his way.

"A horse?" Roxanne said when Shiloh's father managed to call. Then: "Let's worry about covering the child support before we go adding complications. Besides, it's easy to break your neck, falling off a horse."

Listening in bed, Shiloh thought about the true movie they'd seen at church called *The Joni Erickson Story,* where a girl dove into a lake and hit her head on a rock at the bottom. When she didn't come back up, and her friends went in after her, she'd broken her neck and was paralyzed and had to learn to write with a pen between her teeth. After the movie, Shiloh had tried this, forming large, shaky letters across the back of a bulletin until her mother made her quit.

It was January, and still dark out in the early mornings when Shiloh's mother dropped her off at the Peels'. They'd been watching Shiloh for a month, now, before and after school, while Roxanne worked her new office-manager job at the medical clinic. All six Peels—and one on the way—would be sleeping upstairs when Shiloh got there, but Mr. Peel left the front door unlocked and a lamp on in the living room so she could come on in and read, quietly. Each morning, she crept through the living room to the dining room, where the table was cluttered with empty lunch-boxes, or schoolbooks, or sometimes even dingy white laundry to be folded. Against the wall, the large aquarium that held the turtles sat on an old steamer trunk. They were bluish green, the size of silver dollars, and they nudged themselves over and under each other in an inch of murky water. Shiloh liked how they scraped at the glass on the side of the tank with their thick, wrinkly feet. How they ducked into their shells when she touched them and then poked their heads out slowly, like they were getting used to her. Andrea Peel, who was in fourth grade like Shiloh, was raising the turtles for 4-H. She never cleaned the aquarium, and Shiloh had scraped the words "wash me" in the scum inside to remind her. Sometimes the Peels' orange cat reached in a long paw, and days later a turtle would turn up in a dark corner or behind the couch. Once Shiloh had found one wedged under the refrigerator, nearly dried out but still alive.

Some mornings Shiloh tiptoed upstairs and peered in at the sleeping Peels. Mr. and Mrs. Peel slept in the room at the end of the hall, Mr. Peel on his back, snoring through his mustache, and Mrs. Peel on her side, hand on her round, pregnant belly. She was seven months along, and always shifted around on the bed like she was waking up. The twins—five-year-old towheaded boys—slept in the room on the right, twisted up in their sheets on a pair of single beds. Andrea shared the room across the hall with Janice, who was thirteen. The house had once been divided into apartments, and the girls' room was floored with linoleum and had its own sink and set of cupboards.

Andrea was a shy, narrow-faced girl who picked her scabs. Awake, she sometimes seemed to be holding her breath, which made Shiloh want to poke her in the stomach to get her started again. Asleep, her mouth stayed open and her breathing was loud. The longer Shiloh stood over her, the more Andrea's upper lip did its rabbity twitching. She and Andrea were supposed to be friends, but they weren't. Shiloh liked to pretend she could add things to Andrea's dreams—creepy things, like hands with long, razor fingernails, or embarrassing things, like having an accident at school. Then she'd touch the sleeping girl's flat blond hair so that she jerked in her sleep, sometimes moaning in dismay.

"Did you come in my room?" Andrea asked more than once, shuffling down the stairs in her slippers and staring with pale blue eyes at Shiloh, who by that time would be reading in Mr. Peel's recliner. The chair smelled just like him—Dial soap and oranges.

"No," Shiloh said. "You must have been dreaming."

After school, Shiloh liked to follow Janice Peel upstairs and through the old draperies that had been strung across the middle of the room to divide it. She sat on the floor near the bed while Janice took Shiloh's fuzzy blond hair out of its ponytail and tried various strategies for making it behave. Beside the bed was a wallet-sized photo of Ben, Janice's boyfriend from church, whose lip caught on the pointy upper tooth that seemed to have grown outside the row.

"We don't kiss," Janice said when Shiloh asked. "He respects me too much. He's going to be a minister." Janice had a long brown braid, a plain face, and was on her way to what Shiloh's mother called a pear-shaped figure. Around her neck she wore a gold-toned cross Ben had given her.

Shiloh nodded. There were ministers everywhere in this town, because of the seminary. Mr. Peel had moved his family here from Ohio so he could study to be a minister, but he and Mrs. Peel kept having babies, and he'd had to go back to work as a pharmacist's assistant. Shiloh and her mother went to church on Sundays, but the Peels took things to a whole new level.

"Don't you want to kiss him, though?" Shiloh said.

"Not really," Janice said. She punched a button on her cassette player and played Journey's "Open Arms," turning the volume down low because secular music wasn't allowed.

Andrea, just home from her piano lesson, poked her face through the curtain.

"Out," Janice said.

"Janice is telling me a secret," Shiloh said. She tried to say it nicely.

"I'm not telling a secret. You just can't come in."

"Shiloh's in."

"It's my room."

"It's all of ours house, though."

Janice flipped her long braid over her shoulder and stared Andrea down.

"What would Jesus do?" said Andrea.

"Out," said Janice again.

Andrea let the curtain close and retreated across the bedroom floor, her tennis shoes squeaking on the linoleum.

The singer belted out the chorus. Shiloh had considered this song before, as it was also a favorite of her stepsister, Cheryl. "This song could be really dirty," said Shiloh, "if it said 'open legs' instead of 'open arms.'" She began to sing, softly. "So, now I come . . . to you . . . with ohhh . . . pen . . . legs."

Janice giggled wickedly.

"So, here I am . . . with ohhh . . . pen legs," Shiloh sang.

"I'm going to tell you're listening to dirty music," said Andrea from across the room.

"What would Jesus do?" Shiloh said.

When Mrs. Peel had to go on bed rest, Shiloh's mother explained about the stitches, down there. Every time Shiloh thought about this she got a pain that made her cross her legs as hard as she could. At the Peels', Janice had to take over making dinner for the family, and Shiloh spent more and more time in the backyard with Andrea and the twins. They played war, mostly, and since Kentucky had been borderland, Shiloh made one of the twins Confederate and one of them Union. She made herself general— sometimes Sherman and sometimes Lee—and she directed battle with sticks for guns and split firewood for cannons. Her father discussed weapons sometimes, but mainly he talked about his two favorite things: tactics and personality. "Brother against brother," Shiloh intoned while the boys whacked Whiffle Bats. Every battle ended when one twin recognized the other by his minor birth defect, a thin web of skin between the third and fourth fingers of his left hand. The Lord had made him that way, so the Peels had never had it fixed.

Andrea always did exactly what Shiloh said, playing war widow over by the garage, wringing her hands and waiting for the return of her man. It should have made Shiloh like her more, but didn't. One afternoon, Shiloh got fed up and aimed her stick at Andrea, right under the waist of her hand-me-down blue parka. Andrea just kept wringing her hands. "I shot you in the base of the spine," Shiloh explained. "Now you're paralyzed, which means you can't move."

"I know what it means," Andrea said. "Like Joni Erickson." She lay down, splayed out her legs, and slapped the ground with her feet.

"Now just stop moving," Shiloh said.

Andrea stopped. "What happens now?"

"Now you're a captive. You wait for the army to collect you." Shiloh nudged Andrea's leg with her foot. "Can you feel that?"

"Yes."

"You're supposed to say no."

"No."

"I'll be right back," Shiloh said. She headed inside to pee, leaving Andrea staring up at the sky and the twins stockpiling old walnuts for cannonballs. Mr. Peel, home from work early, sat at the kitchen table doing figures with a pencil. He smiled at Shiloh, then rubbed something out with his pink eraser. In the living room, Janice was propping Mrs. Peel's swollen feet up with throw pillows. As Shiloh crossed the dining room to the downstairs bathroom, she saw something dark edging across the rug. She squatted and set one finger in front of the turtle for it to crawl over. "Turtle got out," she said as Janice passed her on the way to the kitchen.

Janice rolled her eyes and kept on going. In a minute, she popped her head back in. "Where's Andrea? I need her to peel potatoes."

"I'll do it," said Shiloh.

"It's Andrea's job," Janice said. Shiloh listened to the whoosh of the gas stove coming on. She listened to Mrs. Peel groaning softly on the couch as she switched sides. The turtle wanted to crawl up into Shiloh's hand, and she let it. She glanced toward the kitchen, then toward the living room. Then she deposited it in the pocket of her parka.

Outside, the twins had started kicking a ball against the garage door, but Andrea still lay flat on her back.

"You can come in now," Shiloh called.

Andrea stayed put. The sky was getting dark, and the air felt solid and cold. Past the barbed-wire fence at the back of the yard, the ground had been broken for condominiums. Chunks of red clay spilled across what was left of the dead grass. They couldn't make the Peels move, so they were building around them.

Shiloh crossed the yard halfway. "You don't have to lay there anymore."

Andrea lifted her head. "I can't move," she said. "You have to drag me back to the house."

Shiloh put her hands on her hips. "Janice says for you to come inside." She walked the rest of the way to Andrea and stood looking down at her. She moved her hands to her pockets and fingered the tiny turtle.

"I'm on bed rest." Andrea's nose was running and she turned her head sideways, trying to wipe it into the hood of her coat without moving her arms.

"Bed rest hurts," Shiloh said.

"I'm on *ground* rest," Andrea amended.

"Bed rest hurts like when you have to pee," Shiloh said. The thought of it made her clamp her legs tightly together. "They take a needle and thread and stitch you closed where the baby comes out. Ask someone. Ask your mom." Shiloh's hand snuck down between her legs. She couldn't help it.

"You're not supposed to touch yourself there," Andrea said, looking past Shiloh to the house.

"I didn't," said Shiloh, and she snatched back her hand.

THE NEXT NIGHT, while Shiloh was watching television, Mr. Peel called.

Roxanne covered the mouthpiece with her hand. "Mr. Peel wants to know if you've seen one of Andrea's turtles. He wondered if it crawled into some of your things."

"I saw one," Shiloh said, "but I put it back."

"Shiloh, look at me." Shiloh put on her most serious face and looked at her mother. The turtle was in a Tupperware container under her bed, where she could check on it in the middle of the night. She had named it Traveler, after General Lee's horse. She was going to take it with her when she visited her dad. "Andrea thinks you might have it," Roxanne said. "I'm on edge tonight, so tell me straight."

"Has she checked under the refrigerator?"

Roxanne blinked at her. She took her hand off the mouthpiece. "We'll keep our eyes open, Bob. How're you holding up?" Then Roxanne stretched the phone cord into her bedroom, and Shiloh turned down the volume to see if she could hear, but she couldn't.

The next morning, before any of the Peels woke up, Shiloh laid Traveler gently behind the downstairs toilet, where Janice Peel spied him as she was washing her face. Later, in front of the aquarium, Mr. Peel stood Andrea before Shiloh and said, "I think someone owes someone an apology."

"It's okay," Shiloh said.

"It's not okay," said Mr. Peel. "It's important to give people the benefit of the doubt." He moved his hands up and down Andrea's arms, like he was warming her up.

Andrea's bangs rose from her forehead with static electricity. She looked toward Shiloh's knees and said, "Sorry."

"How about a hug?" Mr. Peel said. Shiloh stepped forward and put her arms around Andrea. Andrea hugged back, but when they released each other, her face looked stormy.

"I wanted to take the turtle, but I didn't," Shiloh said. This felt truthful.

"Maybe Andrea will even give you a turtle once her project is over." Mr. Peel shook Andrea's shoulder. "What do you say?"

"Maybe."

"There you go," said Mr. Peel. "Shiloh, I like your sweet spirit of forgiveness. Andrea, I like your generous heart. You girls are going to be just fine."

SHILOH'S OWN FATHER believed that love meant never having to say you're sorry. Her mother said that was a stupid philosophy from a stupid book, but her father said that when people loved each other, they told each other their reasons for doing things, and everyone understood, even if it felt bad. Every month he came to pick up Shiloh in his painter's van and they drove the fifty miles to his newly built house. He always started out asking about school and ended up talking about divorce.

"Your mother and I weren't working out," he said. "She's kind of intense, but that has nothing to do with you. And I'm still your father." He raised one dark eyebrow, then another, as if he was telling the punch line to a joke. He made a lot of faces these days, trying to make her laugh. "We understand each other, right?"

"Right."

"And besides, you're not losing a father, you're gaining a family."

"I know."

It was already mid-February and nearly dusk. The days were growing longer. The muddy fields rolled out from the road into the distance, and the cows bumped along home together, all in the same direction. Soon the road wound around a hill where four abandoned whiskey warehouses leaned into the slope like old men. This meant they were getting close to her father's new house. "Can we go out to eat?" Shiloh said. "Before we get there?"

"Of course not. Jill has dinner ready. Cheryl and Mark are looking forward to seeing you."

Shiloh felt her stomach turn over. She tried not to think about Cheryl and Mark until she had to, and now she had to.

"Everyone's just adjusting," her father said. "You and Cheryl and Mark—pretty soon you're all going to get along just fine. Change isn't bad, Shiloh. It all depends on the tack you take. Okay?"

"Okay," Shiloh said.

At supper, she sat between her step-siblings. They were dark-complected kids with their mother's brown eyes and square jaw, and around them, Shiloh had trouble remembering what she looked like. She could touch her ponytail, but her face felt like a smudge. While Jill dished up mashed potatoes and slippery piles of lima beans, she asked what Shiloh wanted for her birthday. At home, Shiloh was not allowed to say what she wanted, because it was rude. She looked at her dad, who looked at his watch.

"Five-twenty-two and it's still light out," he said.

"We can see that," Cheryl said, rolling her eyes.

"I know what she wants for her birthday," said Shiloh's father. "A certain four-legged creature."

"A horse," Mark said. Then he elbowed Shiloh hard and whispered, "Say you want a horse."

Jill put her fork down and blinked slowly at Shiloh's father.

"What?" he said.

"We've discussed this," Jill said through her teeth. "My friend Pat says it costs four hundred dollars a year in carrots alone. Not to mention we'd have to build a barn or shed."

"Does that sound logical to you? Do you realize how many carrots that is?"

"We're not getting a horse?" Mark said.

Jill looked at Shiloh's father like he made her tired.

"You can break your neck, falling off a horse," Shiloh said, and they all stopped chewing and stared at her.

"You are so weird," said Cheryl.

"Is your food okay, Shiloh?" said Jill.

Shiloh's plate was a mess of lima beans she'd tried to hide in her potatoes. She hated lima beans, the way they broke open into mushiness when she chewed.

"Succotash," her father said, pointing, "helped fuel the Union army. Sherman walked twelve miles a day with his army on succotash. On his march to the sea."

"I bet he had a horse," Mark said.

"Sherman thought you could get things over with as quickly as possible or you could pussyfoot around feeling bad and make things last longer. Better to get it over with quick. Like pulling off a Band-Aid. Sherman would have eaten his lima beans first."

Shiloh took a bite and tried not to breathe through her nose, but she could still taste.

"Sherman had to do a lot of things he didn't want to do," Shiloh's father went on. "Killing people, burning houses, ruining food so people would get hungry and give up faster. 'War is war,'" Shiloh's father recited, directing the words with his fork, "'and you cannot refine it.'"

"Did he paralyze people?" said Shiloh.

"Eat," said her father.

"If we were paralyzed," Shiloh said, "we'd have to suck up our food through a straw."

"Yeah, but we're not." Cheryl smirked at Mark. "God."

Before bed, Mark and Cheryl kissed Jill good night, then they kissed Shiloh's father good night, too, as if they'd always known him. Shiloh did not kiss Jill good night, but Jill seemed not to notice. Her mother sometimes asked her if she'd kissed Jill, and Shiloh wanted to be able to say no. When she kissed her father good night, she felt like she was copying Mark and Cheryl, even though she was the one who had been kissing him good night for years. This made her miss him, a little, even though he was right there in front of her.

The kids brushed their teeth together in the upstairs bathroom. Shiloh let Mark and Cheryl spit first, saving her spit until last so they couldn't watch. Mark turned on the water when he spit, and Cheryl reached over and turned it off. Mark turned it on again; Cheryl turned it off. Then Mark punched Cheryl in the shoulder.

"Didn't hurt," Cheryl said, speaking around her toothbrush. She spit again, then punched Mark in the chest, making her fist with the knuckles pointed. In the mirror, Shiloh saw Mark wince.

"Didn't hurt," he said after a moment, toothpaste foaming at his mouth. He spit hard into the sink and turned the water back on. He took a step back and karate-chopped Cheryl in her lower back, knocking her hips against the counter. She made a low *ugh* sound, but then straightened up and rinsed her toothbrush. "Didn't hurt."

Shiloh's mouth was full. She had to spit, and it was beginning to feel like it would go down the back of her throat. She pressed her lips together.

Mark leaned in to spit and Cheryl's eyes met Shiloh's in the mirror. "What do you think you're looking at?" Cheryl said, and Shiloh swallowed everything in her mouth in a big gulp. "That's disgusting," Cheryl said.

Mark raised his head. "What did she do?"

"Shiloh swallows."

"No, I don't."

"Not what it looked like to me."

"Yeah," said Mark, but just then, on her way out of the bathroom, Cheryl planted a kick to the back of his leg that slammed his knee into the cupboard and knocked him down. He hunched over his leg, whimpering, "Didn't hurt," but Cheryl had already disappeared into her room and closed the door.

All Cheryl had was a single canopy bed, or Shiloh would have had to sleep with her. Mark had bunks. In his room, Shiloh hoisted herself to the top and crawled between the football-print sheets. She tried to breathe slowly, like she was already asleep. The overhead light shone red through her eyelids, but she made herself very still. She lay on her back with her hands down at her sides. Her zip-up red pajamas with the feet in them had become too short and pulled at the crotch. They pushed against Shiloh's chest, too, which felt sore.

Mark entered, shushing his feet along the carpet to make static electricity, and Shiloh prepared herself for the spark of his finger against her cheek. She felt the finger, but this time the spark didn't work. "I know you're awake," he said. Shiloh kept her breathing regular. She imagined that she couldn't move if she wanted to, that she'd lost all feeling in her body from the neck down.

Mark dropped himself onto the lower bunk and flipped off the light switch. He began kicking the bottom of Shiloh's mattress. Her body lifted and settled with each small impact.

"Who do you think your dad likes better," Mark said, "you or me? I mean, I live with him. I see him every day. I'm a live-in kid, *and* I'm a boy."

Shiloh kept so still that her body seemed to be humming.

"I know you can hear me," Mark said.

Shiloh counted to ten. She itched to move, but did not. She counted to one hundred, and the itch went away. Below, Mark began to breathe deeply, whistling through his nose like Shiloh had before the doctor removed her adenoids. Downstairs, her father and Jill were arguing, and their voices mingled with the voices on television.

Soon the television went quiet, and Shiloh heard her father and Jill climb the stairs to their room and close the door. Then she had to pee. She pressed her legs together. She thought about Mrs. Peel's stitches, and she pressed harder, tightening her thighs toward each other. She did not want to risk waking up Mark just to go to the bathroom, but she had a warm feeling between her legs that she thought might be pee coming. It was a kind of glow that started from where the crotch of her pajamas pushed into her, and she moved her legs just a little, crossing them. Then the warmth down there became something throbbing, something that throbbed up her body and made her slide her legs against each other. She opened her mouth and breathed hard into the sheet. She rocked her hips into the feeling and it rose in her, huge, and when it burst into a million separate feelings and fizzled down her arms and legs, she heard herself gasping into the darkness. Afterward, her heart beat in her ears. She was afraid Mark had heard something, but soon his breathing separated itself from the silence. Shiloh's body fell limp. She wondered if she had paralyzed herself. She could still feel the smoothness of the sheet against her hands and feet, but she did not try to move in case she would find out she really was paralyzed, or in case she would find out she wasn't.

THE NEXT MONDAY morning, Shiloh pushed open the Peels' front door to find Mrs. Peel already lying on the couch. Sleep dragged her face into grooves—between her eyes, under her eyes, on either side of her mouth. Her hair looked dirty, and her skin was shiny as raw chicken. Then her eyes popped open, and Shiloh stepped back.

"What can I do for you, Shiloh?" Mrs. Peel said, in a voice that let Shiloh know that the woman had been awake, waiting for her. A plastic tube snuck from under her shirt and disappeared into a fanny pack around her waist.

"Are you okay?"

"Uncomfortable," said Mrs. Peel. "But otherwise just fine. Maybe you can wait in the kitchen this morning." Mrs. Peel turned her face to the back of the couch and sighed.

The turtles were absolutely still in their shells. Shiloh doubted they had even been fed, so she raised the lid and sprinkled in plenty of food, letting out a moist green smell, like growing things. She watched them for a while, thinking that she didn't blame them for tucking into themselves when their tank was such a mess. Then she sat at the kitchen table, copying a drawing of a turtle from a book—*Terrapins of North America*—until Mr. Peel shuffled into the kitchen in his slippers and plaid robe. He had already loaded the four-slot toaster with bread before he noticed Shiloh. "Hey, there," he said. "I guess it's Monday."

At home she'd eaten a granola bar, but she took the toast Mr. Peel offered, anyway. He'd buttered it himself.

"How's that mother of yours," Mr. Peel said. "Still playing the guitar?"

"She's getting pretty good," Shiloh said. Mr. Peel sat down across from her. "Why does Mrs. Peel have a tube?"

"It's just a little pump for medicine. Just a little extra help keeping the baby in. Mrs. Peel's body wants it to be time, but it's not. We're just trusting the Lord that everything will be okay." Mr. Peel sounded patient, but there was something about the way he said "Mrs. Peel's body," like the body was separate from Mrs. Peel, like it was an appliance they'd bought at Sears that was turning into more trouble than it was worth.

"My dad's getting me a horse," Shiloh said.

"That a fact." Mr. Peel lay a long finger over his mustache and drew it slowly downward. "He must be quite a dad."

Andrea appeared in the kitchen and moved to the table to stand against her father, pressing her face into his shoulder. "You're *my* dad," she said in a baby voice. Shiloh waited for Mr. Peel to tell her to grow up, but he just put his hand on her hair.

From the living room, Mrs. Peel called, "Bob," in a low, moaning voice, and Mr. Peel pushed back his chair and stood up. Andrea clung to his legs.

"Sweetie," he said, "sit here with Shiloh and eat my toast. Coming, Mrs. Peel."

"How come your dad calls your mom 'Mrs. Peel'?" Shiloh asked when Mr. Peel left the room.

"He can call her whatever he wants," said Andrea. "She's his wife and he's her husband."

"I know, but why does he? My parents call each other 'Roxanne' and 'Fred.' Or they say, 'your mother' and 'your father.'"

"Your parents aren't married anymore."

"Yeah," Shiloh said, "but when they were married he called her 'Honey.' And he calls my stepmother 'Baby,' or 'Jill.'"

From the living room, Mrs. Peel said, "No, no, not that way," and Mr. Peel said, "Sorry."

"Does your mom like being pregnant?" Shiloh asked.

Andrea shrugged. She took a bite of toast and held it in her mouth without chewing. Her light blue eyes seemed brighter, like she was coming down with something.

"Does your dad like it when your mom's pregnant?"

Andrea stared at the piece of toast she held. Her hand started to shake.

"Maybe she shouldn't get pregnant so much," Shiloh

whispered. "Maybe that's why he calls her 'Mrs. Peel.'"
She knew she was being mean, but there was nothing mean
about the words she was saying. Something else in the room
was making them mean.

Andrea wiped her nose with the sleeve of her bath-
robe, and Shiloh handed her a napkin. "You shouldn't wipe
your nose on your clothes," she told her.

After school, Shiloh collected an armful of kindling and
some two-by-fours from the woodpile, and she and the
twins laid down a train track from the back door to the
middle of the yard and around the walnut tree. The twin
with the merged fingers stepped along the track as the
Confederate train, while Shiloh and the other twin hid
behind the tree to ambush him. When Andrea came home
from her piano lesson, she stood out on the back stoop,
watching, then began walking on the tracks, not carefully
at all, shifting the sticks out of line.

"You're going to get ambushed if you stay on those
tracks," Shiloh said.

"They don't even look like railroad tracks," Andrea
said, though she started walking more carefully.

Shiloh moved to the crumbling driveway and hurled a
fist-sized piece of broken concrete at part of the track several feet away from Andrea. The sticks scattered and the
twins cheered.

Shiloh lobbed another rock. "Our mission has changed.
We have to bust up this track so bad that the whole Confederate army can't put it back together." The twins started

kicking the sticks in all different directions, while Andrea stood still. "You can bust it up, too," Shiloh said. "We're just not playing train anymore, that's all. We're playing demolition."

Andrea started kicking reluctantly at the tracks. Shiloh selected a two-by-four the length of her arm and balanced it on a rock. She set an old, hardened walnut on one end of the board, and slammed the other end with her fist. The walnut sailed too far—over the tracks, over Andrea—and smacked into the garage wall, breaking open. The next walnut skittered up onto the roof of the garage and rolled back down. The twins and Andrea gathered around Shiloh.

"I bet we could send one over the house," Shiloh said. "Run out front and see."

Andrea set off for the front yard, and one of the twins handed Shiloh another walnut. She turned the launcher toward the house, and the next walnut thwacked close to the back door with enough force to dent the aluminum siding. In three seconds, Shiloh's mother appeared. "I don't even want to know what that noise was," she said. "Shiloh, now. It's time to leave."

Shiloh followed her mother through the kitchen, dining room, and living room. Inside the Peels' house, Roxanne looked even cleaner than usual. Her hair, her pantsuit— everything was smooth and tucked in. On the couch, Mrs. Peel had pulled down her shirt to cover the tube. She had draped one arm across her forehead, pushing back her thin brown hair.

"You take it easy," Roxanne said to her. "I'll send a

casserole with Shiloh tomorrow. We'll see about some housework, too. You've got your hands full, and Shiloh is a good helper."

"We can manage fine ourselves," Mrs. Peel said, but Roxanne was already out the door.

On the front porch, they met Mr. Peel coming home from work. "Let me know when you head to the hospital," Roxanne said. "I'd be happy to come to the house in a pinch." She folded Mr. Peel's hand in between both of hers. "I'm keeping you all in my prayers."

"Roxanne, that means so much." Mr. Peel reached his free hand down and placed it on top of Shiloh's head. It felt warm and firm, like a lid that fit her exactly. At the corner of the house, the hedge rustled. It was an evergreen with bare spots, from last year's tentworms, and through one of the bare spots Shiloh thought she could see the bright fever of Andrea's eyes.

"WHEN I WAS PREGNANT with you, the doctor kept telling me not to worry about gaining more weight," Roxanne said that night as she wiped down the bathroom scale. She wore a bandanna to hold back her dark hair so that her face showed the perfect oval shape she'd traced, once, with soap, in a mirror for Shiloh. Shiloh was scrubbing the tub with clumpy blue powder and trying not to breathe. The fumes felt like they were scraping out the insides of her head, but Roxanne said it was fine as long as they didn't use ammonia at the same time. "You turned out to be an eight-pounder, but I was back in my clothes by the time you were two months old. Never had to wear a girdle, either, because I always sucked in my stomach. Shiloh?"

Shiloh looked up, and Roxanne had raised her sweatshirt. Her stomach was very pale, with freckles, and her ribs arched over the hollowness, like the entrance to a tunnel. "As I'm walking to my car, I suck in my stomach. As I'm sitting at my desk? Suck in my stomach." Roxanne made a fist and thumped her stomach a few times. Then she lowered her shirt and started scrubbing the toilet lid. "There's only so much you can control, though. Take Jill. You know how her legs get wider under her bottom? Those are saddlebags. Some people are fat there no matter how skinny they are everywhere else. Me? I gain a few, I gain it all over. Proportional. The only way to get rid of fat like Jill's is to have it sucked out with a vacuum."

Roxanne reached down and pinched Shiloh under the butt, and Shiloh scooted away.

"The woman knows how to get what she wants, though, I'll give her that. Let's just say she compensates for her drawbacks with tactical maneuvers. Then there's Marge Peel. Hips as wide as a bus, and the rest of her gone to fat. There's a woman who will never get her body back in a million years."

"And Joni Erickson," Shiloh said. "She'll never get her body back."

Roxanne sucked her bottom lip between her teeth. "I'm glad you brought that up, Shiloh," she said after a moment. "That really puts things into perspective." Roxanne dropped the cleaning rag and folded her hands, as if she were going to pray, and then she closed her eyes and was praying. "Thank you, Lord, for reminding us of what's important. In your name, amen."

Shiloh stared at her.

"I'm really feeling spiritual these days," Roxanne explained.

"Maybe Mrs. Peel's hips are too wide to hold the baby in," Shiloh said.

"No, no, no. Forget I said anything. That's just something that happens sometimes for no reason."

"I'm never having a baby," Shiloh said. "No stitching or tubes, either."

"Don't be melodramatic. That hardly ever happens." Roxanne leaned on the toilet rim, now, scrubbing its underside with an old toothbrush. "And when you grow up you'll want to be close to a man, and after you get married you'll want to be really close to him, and then you'll want to have a baby."

"I won't."

"Trust me," Roxanne said. "It hurts to have a baby, but making one feels good."

"Between your legs?"

Roxanne sat back on her heels. She took the toothbrush out from under the rim of the toilet. "What do you mean?"

Shiloh heard the quiet under the question. "Nothing."

Roxanne pulled her up and sat her on the edge of the

tub. She stuck her face into Shiloh's face. Without her makeup, Roxanne's eyes seemed very small, greenish with tiny spots of brown. "Has anyone touched you there?" Roxanne said. "Anyone at your father's house?"

"No."

Roxanne let out a wet breath that smelled like coffee. "If anyone touches you, or touches themselves in front of you, anything that makes you feel weird, come home and tell me." She clapped her hand to her forehead. "Lord," she started praying again, but then took her hand away and opened her eyes, concentrating again on Shiloh. "Think," she said. "Tell me if anything has happened."

Shiloh tried not to remember the feeling. If she remembered it, she would say it. "Andrea and I were talking about the stitches," she said.

"That's all?"

Shiloh shrugged.

"What, Shiloh. She showed you her privates?"

Shiloh shrugged again. She was afraid to say yes, but she was also afraid to say no.

"I don't know what to do," Roxanne said, blowing out another long breath. "Probably it's natural, with everything that's going on. Probably it's no big deal. But someone should probably let Bob know, just in case."

Shiloh turned back toward the tub. The cleanser had dried and when she began to rinse it she had to scrub again to get it all off. She could feel her mother watching her, still, and she kept her head down, squeezing the sponge and wiping carefully long after the tub was clean, after her mother had finished bleaching the toilet bowl and headed into the hallway to make the call.

FOR THE FOLLOWING TWO WEEKS, Andrea was grounded to her room after school so she could do some thinking about her behavior. When it was time to make dinner, Janice called Shiloh, instead, and Shiloh peeled carrots and thawed chicken in the microwave and heard about how Janice had kissed Ben, finally, and then promptly broken up with him.

"It's not like you'd think," Janice said, whispering because Mrs. Peel was in the next room. "It's wet, and gross, and it feels like you might as well not even be there." She held up a tomato she'd sliced in half. "It's like having your mouth mashed by a tomato, only the tomato gets mad when you don't like it." Ben wasn't even going to be a minister, anymore, either. He was going to play in the NBA.

Spring was coming. The sky hung low with rain that held off, and trees pushed out swollen buds. The stiff green tips of tulip leaves had started poking up through the still-hard ground. Everything was going to bust open, and it was all too much for Mrs. Peel's body. The afternoon her water broke, in late March, Shiloh's mother was waiting at the Peels', having taken off work early to help out.

Roxanne lined everyone up in the living room and said, "Your mother's going to be just fine. The baby's going to be just fine. But now"—and she swept her arm to indicate the collection of cups and bowls by the couch from Mrs. Peel, the food ground into the rug, the heap of dirty shoes by the door—"now is our opportunity to get this place shipshape."

The Peels were silent. Janice watched Roxanne respectfully, Andrea chewed her cuticles, and the twins looked confused.

"Janice, the sweeper," Roxanne said. "Twins, toys and shoes. Everything in its place. You know where everything goes?" The boys nodded. "Good. Let's see who can do the most."

The twins scrambled off, leaving Shiloh and Andrea. Andrea's bangs hung past her eyes, and down the front of her turtleneck a dribble of spaghetti sauce from the night before had hardened into a crust.

"We can clean the tank," Shiloh said, pointing into the dining room.

Roxanne took two steps toward the dining room and made a face. "That's what I smell."

"We can drag it outside and use the hose," Shiloh said.

"I can do it by myself," Andrea said.

"Tell you what," Roxanne said. "You two take care of the tank and then come in and help me with the bathrooms. Then," she said, eyeing Andrea, "we'll clean ourselves up nice for when your mom comes home."

"I don't need help," Andrea said.

"I want to help, though," said Shiloh.

"It'll go much faster with two," Roxanne said. "You'll see."

There was no arguing with Roxanne when her voice got crisp. She peeled off her blazer and hoisted the tank into her arms. She said, "Andrea, the door," and Andrea held open the door while Shiloh followed with paper towels and Windex.

Outside, it felt like spring when you stood in the sun, and winter, still, when you stood in the shade. The yard was strewn with boards as well as the twins' bikes and plastic sports equipment. "Jesus Christ," Shiloh heard Roxanne say under her breath, heaving the tank toward a clear spot. "Praise him," she added when Andrea's head snapped up.

Shiloh set down the paper towels and the Windex and took the lid off the tank. She knelt on the ground, dampening the knees of her jeans. One of the turtles had its legs out, but when she touched it, the legs disappeared back into the shell.

"Go to it," Roxanne said, and returned to the house.

Andrea knelt on the other side of the tank, opposite Shiloh. "Don't touch them," she said.

"I was just making sure they were alive," said Shiloh. "You want them to be alive, don't you?"

"They're alive," said Andrea.

Shiloh wiped her finger up the inside of the glass, and it came away green and gummy. As she glanced around the yard for a pail or a bucket to put the turtles in while they cleaned the tank, she heard the squirt of the Windex bottle and felt a light spray on her arm.

Andrea had sprayed Windex onto the inside of one of the glass panes. Windex ran down toward the green water at the bottom, and Shiloh tore off a paper towel and wiped it up as fast as she could. Ammonia stung the inside of her nose, and soon it was stinging her hand, too, where her skin was dry from cleaning without gloves.

Andrea twisted the spout to high and sprayed again, covering Shiloh's arms and the back of one of the turtles. "Cut it out," Shiloh said, wiping furiously.

Andrea picked up a turtle and held the nozzle right up to where the curved shell met its flat little belly. "Make me," she said, and Shiloh knocked the bottle out of her hand. It hit the ground, and they both reached for it, but Shiloh was faster. She grabbed the bottle and held it behind her back.

"What's your problem? That's *bad* for them."

"They're mine," Andrea said. She planted her tennis shoe against the tank and shoved it a few inches in the dirt.

Shiloh stood up. "We have to have something to put them in first. Don't do anything until I get back." She clutched the Windex bottle and walked backward halfway across the lawn, to make sure Andrea didn't do anything. Andrea didn't. She just scooted away from the tank on her butt and lifted a small plank from a pile. Shiloh turned toward the house and made herself walk normally. Her hands were really stinging now, at the knuckles and fingernails, but she wouldn't rinse them. She would head inside and go right for the Tupperware drawer and be back in two seconds. Maybe she would tell her mother.

But as she drew closer to the back stoop, something landed on the ground behind her with a soft thud. The second turtle smacked the cement foundation of the house, sticking there for half a second before dropping soundlessly to the ground. When Shiloh reached it, she saw the crackled, smashed-in place on its shell, and her throat closed up. Andrea was already loading the launcher again, but the turtle in Shiloh's hands was leaking a thin purple liquid, and Shiloh couldn't seem to move right. She took two steps toward Andrea, as if in slow motion. She lifted her right hand in front of her face, trying to stop things, while she wrapped her left around the broken turtle as if with just the right pressure, held perfectly still, it might grow itself back together and survive.

Invitation

HE TABERNACLE OF the Jackson Ridge camp
meeting was really just a huge metal barn,
with a polished cement floor that sloped down
to an altar and stage. Before services, ushers raised the
five garagelike doors on each sidewall to encourage a cross
draft, and they started up the ceiling fans that droned
electrically twelve feet above the pews. But the cross draft
never amounted to anything much, and the ceiling fans
barely stirred the Kentucky summer air, which settled wetly
on everything like the palpable presence of the Holy Ghost.
In the pews our hair turned frizzy or limp, our skin shone,
and our clothes stuck like Saran Wrap to embarrassing
places, all while we pumped funeral-home fans back and
forth in front of our faces. The fans were fiddle-shaped and
stuck on wooden tongue depressors, and printed on the
back in large black letters were the words *He, with we, can
help you in your time of need.* I wanted to believe it, but the
Jesus on the front of the fans stood pale and slouched,
knocking at a door with a barred window at the top of it—

the door to your heart—like he didn't really expect it to open.

My father had a dual appointment as both minister of the First United Methodist in the town of Jackson and camp-meeting evangelist. Onstage, he drew responses from every section of the audience by lifting his long, graceful arms and adjusting his limber wrists incrementally, at the most important moments. His pale blue eyes could see clear to the back pews where I sat with my older sister, Virginia-Ruth.

"I want you to think about your heart," he said, bringing a thoughtful hand first to his temple, then flat against his chest. We thought about our hearts. "I want you to let its concerns rise to the surface like oil on a road after the rain," he said, and our concerns loosened reluctantly from where we kept them hidden, slipping upward toward a place of exposure.

Our mother always sat up front so she could quiet the crazy woman who walked in late each night and distracted the congregation by shouting out in tongues. My father complained that it threw off his momentum, changed the whole dynamic of his delivery. And, after all, we were United Methodists of the Holiness tradition, not Pentecostals. Some would call this a fine line, but it was 1982, during the tail end of the charismatic movement, and my father believed that certain distinctions were important or things could get out of hand. The Jackson Ridge camp meeting did not encourage chanting or dancing (not even with spirit flags), or barking in the spirit like they did at a church over in Riley, or speaking in tongues.

Every night Virginia-Ruth and I watched for the crazy woman. She always wore the same thick gray sweater over an old red-and-purple-striped dress, even in the heat, and she teetered heavily on spike-heeled sandals. Most women we knew tanned their legs so they could go without hose in the summer, but this woman always wore the same pair of dark stockings, with wide runs that crept up her calves and revealed her skin underneath, white as a raw potato. Her face looked stiff with thick makeup, and she kept her graying hair in a sloppy bun, stabbed through with a pencil. She did not live in town, and was dropped off and picked up each night in an old blue pickup truck that belonged to no one we knew.

Virginia-Ruth and I called her the saved-and-sanctified lady because she always asked us if we were. We avoided her when we could, hustling from the tabernacle and back to the girls' dorm as soon as the invitation to the altar was over. But our parents expected each of us to make a trip to the altar at least once over the course of camp-meeting week, and that was where the woman hovered. Other kids might ignore her, but my sister and I were to be daughterly examples of kindness, even to a woman our parents secretly wished would stop coming. So we nodded and tried not to stare when she asked us her question. We tried not to notice the way she smelled—like something in the refrigerator gone bad, but warmer.

Virginia-Ruth liked to make up stories about the saved-

and-sanctified lady and how she'd lost her mind. "When she was young she was very beautiful," she said, "and this married man, this forty-something loser who owned the only grocery store in town, fell in love with her." This version came early one afternoon, when we were sitting around on the wooden floor of our room with a girl from school named Bonnie. We'd stripped down to our bras and shorts, it was so hot. Virginia-Ruth had positioned herself over by the window fan, and Bonnie lay on her stomach in front of the open door of the miniature refrigerator she'd brought from home, breathing in the cool air. I was even sweatier than they were, since I'd been running around the gravel perimeter of the camp-meeting grounds for the past hour. Lately I'd taken to pushing myself in the heat because sometimes it helped me forget what had become my heart's most secret concern: how, at thirteen, I'd managed to become history's second pregnant virgin.

"The girl worked the cash register at the store, and the man spent entire hours watching her," Virginia-Ruth said. She grinned at me and finished rolling a cigarette, licking the edge of the paper with more tongue than was necessary.

"Which town?" I said.

"Over in Lancaster, but this was a long time ago. You wouldn't have heard about it."

"What did he look like?" Bonnie asked. "I wouldn't mind it if he was nice-looking."

Virginia-Ruth narrowed her eyes, lit her cigarette, and took a slow draw. She took her time, telling stories, and when she exhaled, a little galaxy of smoke meandered toward the fan. Tonight she would be singing in the service, and she said smoking did good things to her sound. I used to smoke, too, until our father found out. Smoking was another way of desecrating your body, the temple of the Lord. In these parts, the sanctity of the temple of the Lord had a lot of pull, and so did our father. He'd made it so you couldn't even buy cigarettes, which was really saying something right in the middle of tobacco country.

And now that I had the baby to consider, smoking was out of the question.

"He wasn't anything special to look at," Virginia-Ruth was saying about the man who'd hired the saved-and-sanctified lady when she was young. "He wasn't really special in any way. He just ran the grocery store. No one could believe it"—here she paused and blinked at Bonnie—"when he killed his wife."

"Maybe the saved-and-sanctified lady did it," I said, on cue. I'd heard this one already. "Maybe that's what pushed her over the edge."

"Yeah, a jealous rage," Bonnie said.

Virginia-Ruth motioned us to quit talking and stretched her neck up to peer out the window. She pinched out her cigarette. We were all supposed to be at the first round of afternoon activities—a basketball shoot-out on the paved cement area beside the boys' dorm, arts and crafts in the Youth Tabernacle, or watching *Herbie, the Love Bug* in the air-conditioned dining hall. Over the low hum of the fan we heard someone crunching toward the dorm on the gravel path. They slammed the screen door downstairs, opened and closed a wooden door, slammed the screen door again, and then crunched away.

"Okay," said Virginia-Ruth. "But it was *not* a jealous rage. The saved-and-sanctified lady wasn't jealous. She wouldn't even give a man like that the time of day. If anything, she felt *sorry* for his wife. But at work he bothered her all the time, always fussing with the register or jerking the strings of the apron he made her wear, so she quit. Then, to prove his love, he beat his wife to death. He *bludgeoned* her. With an *iron*. The girl couldn't live with herself and lost her mind." Virginia-Ruth bowed her head and smiled sadly. At school and church, people were always recruiting her for plays. Everyone said she had great dramatic delivery.

"It's probably chemical or something," Bonnie said. "The lady probably has some kind of chemical imbalance."

"No way," said Virginia-Ruth. She hated practical explanations. She made her face nearly expressionless, like she always did when she was disappointed with people. She turned to the window again, the skin on her chest and neck flushed pink from the heat.

Virginia-Ruth was beautiful. It was something people always said. I used to not pay any attention—she was my sister and she just looked like herself, the way my hand just looked like my hand, not pretty or ugly, just mine. But once last year in the school library, I'd flipped through a book of women movie stars from the thirties and forties. They all looked a little like my sister: large-chested, small-wristed, with dark eyebrows that arched like arrows and mouths that looked ready to say anything, and sometimes a delicate mole like the one on Virginia-Ruth's left cheek that just made everything else look more perfect. Bonnie was pretty, too, but in a thin, blond way. The way Virginia-Ruth looked hit people over the head.

"Virginia-Ruth, I would die for that bra," Bonnie said, trying to change the subject. My sister's disappointment could make you feel sorry.

"They get better," I said. "I mean the stories, not the bras. That's her best bra." Virginia-Ruth had the saved-and-sanctified lady raped at fourteen, impregnated, the baby stolen. Or watching a lover get hit by a train while he struggled to get out of a car that had stalled on the tracks. The saved-and-sanctified lady never went mad from natural causes; she was driven to it.

Virginia-Ruth laughed and cupped her breasts with her hands. Her bra was black, with underwires and padding to make her look bigger. At home she hid it in the bookcase in our room, squeezed between the pages of our thick illustrated Bible from when we were kids. "Martha thinks it's sinful," she said. "Don't you, Martha?"

I shrugged and held my tongue. Virginia-Ruth was older, but she did not have my respect for consequences. All I'd ever said to her about the bra was that I thought Ray Weaver was lusting when he knelt beside her at a service earlier in the week, when she got her one altar trip out of the way. In our afternoon seminar for spiritual women, we'd been reminded to always examine our hearts and our clothes for anything that might encourage lust in men.

Men were not fully in control of their bodies. At the altar, Virginia-Ruth had been wearing a sleeveless blouse, and Ray had bent his head low in prayer, eyes close to a gaping arm-hole, nose nearly grazing the side of one uplifted breast.

Virginia-Ruth had no idea how easy conception could be. I'd thought about telling her I was pregnant, but I thought she might laugh. And even some part of *me* wondered if I was being ridiculous. But I'd missed three periods; there'd been a round, wet spot on the front of Wallace Walker's jeans where he'd pushed against me under my skirt in the church janitorial closet, and the crotch of my panties had been damp with something I knew had to be semen.

During the seminar for spiritual women, I'd sweated it out for some indication that sperm couldn't swim through blue jeans and underwear, but nobody addressed this. In-stead, our youth leader's wife told us how she'd been rebel-lious as a teen, messing around with boys, the whole nine yards. She'd thought she was safe because she never went all the way, but a boy she was with touched himself, then touched her, and she got pregnant. She'd held up each of her index fingers, as if she and the boy had poked each other quickly and retreated. She didn't say if they touched skin-to-skin or only through their clothes.

"I don't get that whole lust thing," Bonnie was saying. "If a guy wants to look at you it's a sin?"

"He can look at you, but if he looks at you and thinks about sex, he's in sin. Unless you're in wedlock." Virginia-Ruth turned and lay down on the floor, her feet on the bed and her head near my knees. Her breasts flattened out.

"So how is the guy supposed to know if he's sinned?" asked Bonnie. "Is it if he gets a hard-on?"

"That's the physical manifestation," I said.

"And you're in sin as a woman," said Virginia-Ruth, speaking straight up to the ceiling, "if something you had on, or some way you were walking, made it happen. If you worry about that kind of thing. Martha worries about that kind of thing. Don't you, Martha?"

Sometimes Virginia-Ruth said I had a conscience big enough for both of us, and other times she said I had an underdeveloped sense of *so what*. But mostly, even though she'd been drunk, once, and she'd also let a guy feel her up, she didn't lord it over me like some people would. And she didn't make fun of me for the lines I wouldn't cross. Like how I never took the Lord's name in vain. When I tried it once, spitting out the words "Jesus Christ" in disgust, it felt so awful that I tried to punish myself by chewing aspirin. Every sin was a hammer blow to the nails in Jesus' hands, and as I vomited I pictured his loving, disappointed face wrenching with new pain. Virginia-Ruth had heard me, and she came into the bathroom and wiped me off and made me drink iced tea until the aspirin taste was gone.

"What I don't get," said Bonnie, "is how you're supposed to feel if a boy kisses you and doesn't think about sex. It's an insult."

I was getting chill bumps, and I pulled my T-shirt on over my head. I wondered what Wallace thought about while he was bumping up against me. His parts had seemed like the hard little head of a cat, butting into the palm of

your hand to be petted. I'd been thinking about the dia-
grams from *Becoming Godly Women;* then Wallace was saying,
"Oh, shit," and, "Sorry," and it was over. This summer he
was in Michigan with his dad. Once I'd talked to him on the
phone but my voice sounded like it was coming through my
nose. He was nice, but it was hard to feel natural. I couldn't
imagine having to tell him we were expecting.

I looked down at my stomach and pushed it out, then
sucked it in. I wondered what I would do when I began to
show.

"Problem?" Virginia-Ruth asked, looking at me looking
at my stomach.

"No," I said. I pulled my knees up in front of me and
tried not to breathe.

Bonnie frowned and picked her toenails. "So what
should a guy be thinking about when he's kissing? Say Jesus
was kissing someone—what would he be thinking about
since he couldn't think about sex? Why else would you kiss
anyone?"

"Jesus never kissed anyone or thought about sex," I
told her.

"How do you know? How do you know he didn't have
wet dreams about Mary whatever-her-name-is—not his
mother, but the other one?"

"I think he did," said Virginia-Ruth. "The whole point
is that he was God and he was a man, and how could a man
not think about sex?"

"Jesus was sinless," I said. "He wasn't married. If he
had sexual thoughts, he didn't dwell on them. Maybe what

counts is how hard you try not to think about it." I got up from the floor and lay down on my bed and pushed my feet against the bottom of the top bunk. "Do you really think you can get pregnant without going all the way?"

"Oh, God," said Bonnie. "They tell you all that so you're scared to mess around."

Virginia-Ruth peered up at me. "Something on your mind?"

"No."

"One in a million chances," said Bonnie. "One in two million."

"What if God wants to punish you?" I reached up and grabbed under my knees, stretching my lower back. "What if He wants to shame you out of fornicating, so He makes you pregnant? He made Mary pregnant. What if to punish you He makes you pregnant with the Antichrist?" I was feeling sick to my stomach. I felt something moving around under my ribs.

Virginia-Ruth sat up and reached under the bed for her roll-on deodorant. "Why are you so uptight about this? You shouldn't run when it's so hot if it goes to your head and makes you all panicky." While she spoke, she prepared another cigarette, holding her elbows out awkwardly to let her deodorant dry. "Martha used to pull big clumps of her hair out when she was in kindergarten. In all our family pictures from that year, Martha has these little bare patches in her hair. She was worried she'd pee her pants even though her classroom had its own bathroom. She kept asking at night, 'But what if someone's in there and I can't wait?'"

I still pulled at my hair, sometimes, but I could usually catch myself. The past two months I'd begun grinding my teeth, though, and that was worse because I did it in my sleep. The dentist told me to stop thinking so hard, and he gave me a U-shaped piece of plastic to bite during the night.

I might have said something to Virginia-Ruth about my problem if Bonnie hadn't been staying with us, but I might not have. When I stood up I felt a little dizzy. I sat back down and put my head between my legs.

"Take a shower for godsakes," Virginia-Ruth said. "You'll feel better." With the blood rushing to my head, her voice sounded like it was coming from a long ways away.

THAT NIGHT AT THE service Bonnie and I sat in the middle pew section near the aisle. Down front, in the pew section to my right, my mother had her hand on the shoulder of the saved-and-sanctified lady. Virginia-Ruth sat alone in the choir loft behind the pulpit, her head and shoulders rising above the enclosure. Her fan was out of sight, but you could see her bangs lift and fall, lift and fall, as she sat through the message. I thumbed through a hymnal, its worn pages soft as a bedsheet, and read through the suggested prayers in the back. Then I read through the suggested wedding and funeral services. I was trying to block out the voice resounding in the back of the tabernacle, to pretend that it didn't belong to my father and that it couldn't sneak in and evacuate my heart. When I came across the infant-dedication service, though, I had to shut the book.

My father was finishing up his Christian-marriage message, and by now I knew the words as well as he did. Husbands should put their wives before themselves, like Christ loved sinners. Wives should invite Jesus into every part of the home, from preparing meals to talking to children about their bodies. Wedlock was a sanctified triangle, with two people pure of body and spirit on the bottom and Christ at the top, so that as the people grew closer together, they would also grow closer to Christ. My father constructed a triangle with his hands and forearms, to demonstrate.

When he took his seat behind the pulpit, my mother shifted in her pew to watch Virginia-Ruth walk from the choir loft to the front of the stage. So far, the saved-and-sanctified lady had been subdued. Just after the opening prayer, she'd offered one loud phrase in tongues, and when my mother gripped her shoulder and whispered in her ear, she quieted down. But my father's use of the word "sanctified" set her off again. Now, in the silence before Virginia-Ruth began her song, the saved-and-sanctified lady began to cry. My mother gave her a tissue, and the woman sniffed loudly, folded it, and stuck it in the collar of her dress like she was saving it for an even more tearful occasion.

Virginia-Ruth was calm. She had good posture. She smiled and waited to start until she was ready, until everyone was quiet and aware that she was in control, and then, without even a cue, she hit us with the first note. She sang a capella, and by the time she finished the first verse of "How Great Thou Art," other women were dabbing at their eyes, too.

I looked at the way my mother was sitting, stiff with pride and with the attempt to keep her face humble. At one point in her life she'd wanted to be a professional singer herself, but the Lord called her to be a minister's wife, and she said she never really had the stage presence, anyway.

I remembered how in our room at night when we were little, she would say that someday boys would want to touch us and that if we let them—which was our decision because of free will—we'd be sorry one day when we met someone we wanted to marry in purity.

I smoothed the dress I'd borrowed from Virginia-Ruth over my knees. The material was white with blue squares. I stared across the tabernacle at the side of my mother's face. I imagined saying, *Mom, I'm pregnant,* and I had to close my eyes because Virginia-Ruth was soaring through the refrain, and my mother's chin had started quivering. I propped my arm on the armrest and fanned myself hard. When a girl in town named Shirl Pepper had her baby at sixteen, my mother said it was sad for the family, for Shirl, who would always have *a past,* and of course it was a sin, so it was sad for God. She'd taken the family three-bean casserole and babysat once a week while Shirl finished high school. The commendable thing, my mother said, was that

Shirl told her parents, and that she stayed in school. But it was easier to find the commendable thing when it was someone else's daughter abusing the gift of free will.

Virginia-Ruth's last note was still echoing through the tabernacle as she returned to her seat in the choir loft. Reverend Hanson, pastor of a different church in Jackson, stepped to the pulpit. He was a short, thick man, who adjusted the microphone to his height and then changed his mind and lifted it out of its holster so he could pace the stage. His wet breath crashed from the sound system like waves, but the nights he delivered the invitation held the camp-meeting records for bringing people down to the altar.

Reverend Hanson raised his hands. "And the people said?"

All of us people said, "Amen."

"And the people said?" he asked again.

"Amen." It was a small roar.

"Who is Jesus calling tonight?" he said softly. He was good at raising and lowering his voice so that you had to listen closely to get what was most important. If my father brought secret concerns to the surface, this man compelled you to confess them so you could clear the way for more concerns you hadn't even thought of yet. "Let's continue in our attitude of praise with hymn number two-twenty-six, 'Softly and Tenderly Jesus Is Calling.'" He paused while the organist found the page. "Some of you must not leave this place tonight without talking to Jesus. You know who you are. You know why you're here. You know I'm talking to you, even if no one else has any reason to know. Sing with me."

When we got to the chorus, "Come home, come home, ye who are weary come home," which really meant come to the altar, I *was* feeling weary. I sat down.

"Are you okay?" Bonnie asked.

"I feel sick to my stomach," I said, and as I said it, I did. I felt sick to my stomach knowing that my life was about to change forever.

"I'll leave with you, if you want," she said. In the past we'd used sickness as an excuse to cut out early. Sometimes the altar calls took over an hour.

"I better not," I said. I was feeling something. I wondered if it was the Holy Spirit, which could make you cry or shake. I felt shaky.

Two girls from the dorm went down the aisle, their arms around each other. Then four adults went down in a stuttering, single-file line. My father knelt between two of them, their heads all bent close, their hands clasped together on the altar like they were warming themselves over a tiny fire. My mother rose from her pew to join him, and some of our youth counselors gathered toward the front to smile gravely in our direction.

I tried to think it all through. If the Holy Spirit was telling me to go down to the altar and I didn't go, what would happen? Would I definitely become pregnant even if I wasn't already? God wasn't supposed to be bound by time. On the other hand, if I was pregnant and confessed it, maybe Jesus would make me not pregnant anymore, but how would I know if that's what had done it? If I was pregnant and I stayed pregnant, everyone was going to find out about it, anyway. It might be better if I confessed before I began to show. If I just got pregnant without any warning, people would assume that fornicating was something I did all the time.

Reverend Hanson went right into "Just As I Am," and between the refrain where we sang, "O Lamb of God, I come, I come," and the new verses, he would speak.

"Jesus has laid something on my heart," he said. "One of you has yet to come. Jesus, help this little one, this youth." Reverend Hanson raised his hands, closed his eyes, and we started a new verse.

A youth. I looked around me. A junior-high boy went down, thin shoulders hunched, a diamond of sweat spreading across the back of his shirt. My stomach hurt.

"Another has yet to come," said Reverend Hanson over the refrain. "Don't forsake the Lord. Something's been weighing on your heart. Each time you refuse Him, you make your heart a little harder."

I was sweating, too. If I told my mother at the altar, maybe since we were in church and in front of people, she wouldn't cry.

I didn't think I'd made a decision, but I felt myself rising to my feet, pulling my skirt away from where it stuck to the backs of my legs, brushing aside Bonnie's hand. I stumbled down the aisle.

"Someone here, tonight, needs relief from a burden," Reverend Hanson was saying.

I passed where the saved-and-sanctified lady was sitting and knelt at an empty section of the altar. My mother, speaking softly with someone in front of the pulpit, saw me. She whispered something to my father, and they smiled at each other. And then it was strange, because I saw my mother approaching slowly, her heels catching every few steps on the carpet, and I sensed, at the same time, someone making their way toward me down the cement aisle to my back. When my mother looked up from her feet, she seemed alarmed, and I knew who it had to be.

I put my hands over my face and waited. When they'd both reached me, I heard my mother whisper, "This is my daughter. I have to pray with her." She knelt on my left and put a possessive arm around my shoulders.

Then the woman sank to the altar on my right, and my mother's perfume mixed with the woman's particular odor. Between my fingers I looked up to where Virginia-Ruth was sitting, but the pulpit blocked my view. I planted my chin on my chest while the woman leaned behind me and wheezed at my mother, "I have to ask her." I felt her damp hand on the center of my back, below my mother's arm.

My mother exhaled through her teeth, fighting to keep her cool. I folded my arms on the altar and buried my head in the crook of my elbow. When I peeked to my right, I saw that tears were streaming down the face of the saved-and-sanctified lady.

"Someone will pray with you," my mother said. "Go and ask my husband." She pressed the woman's hand into my back.

"Mom," I croaked into the altar. "I have to say something."

The woman to my right started whispering. Words I couldn't understand, full of l's and u's and punctuated by clicks, began to roll off the back of her tongue in a wild, slippery song. Her voice rose. Several people praying at the other end of the altar looked up.

"Gol-darn it," my mother said under her breath.

The woman broke off her tongues and began to bite her lips, hard. A spot of blood appeared, swelled, then spilled down her chin. She pointed at my mother and loudly asked if she was saved and sanctified, the words smearing blood across her bottom lip.

"Yes," said my mother, "yes, I am." To me she whispered, "See if you can get her to the bathroom, honey, then come back and pray. I'll find the nurse." She patted my hands.

"Mom," I said, but she rose to her feet. "Mom," I tried again, "I have to tell you something." My voice sounded strained and wobbly and was quickly drowned out by the beginning of a new hymn and by the woman beside me, who'd begun to sob. My mother couldn't hear me, and she walked away up the center aisle, scanning the congregation.

The saved-and-sanctified lady's tears had deposited her makeup in the grooves around her nose. She looked like she was melting. She raised her arms and threw back her head and cried, "Jesus, Jesus, Jesus, Jesus!" each word growing louder. The organist glanced our way and doubled the volume.

Beside me the woman snapped her head up and then dropped it forward, banging her chin on the altar. She rested it there, stunned. Her sobs turned into heavy sighs.

I leaned toward her. Her eyes were red and watery, but focused, and it occurred to me that this woman might be able to look right into my heart. "What did you want to ask me?" I whispered.

I watched her mouth form words, but it was just the silent repetition of her usual question. When she tried to speak she made a small, choking noise.

"Shhh," I said. "It's okay." I stood and took her hand, which was kind of soft and crusty at the same time. I was surprised how easy it was to lead her to the women's restroom beneath the stage. She followed me like a child. I set up a folding chair and sat her in it, and even though her tears stopped, her shoulders kept shaking.

There was a plastic cup under the sink, and I rinsed it out and filled it with water. When I put the cup in her hand, she sipped from it, watching me over the rim.

The building heaved as the congregation started a new hymn. The woman was still watching me. I leaned back against the sink and took a deep breath. "I'm pregnant," I said, the words rising through my throat without my cooperation. It felt like throwing up. "I'm thirteen and I'm not married and I'm pregnant. And I'm a virgin." We both stared at the floor, like the information lay there in a puddle and we were waiting for someone to come along with a mop.

Then the woman blinked up at me and sipped her water. She shook her head and said something into the cup that I couldn't hear.

"What?" I asked, taking the cup from her.

She fingered the skirt of my dress and said, "You've stained yourself."

"Yes," I said, hanging my head. I thought of how in the Bible they made lepers call out, "Unclean, unclean," whenever anyone approached them; then I thought of *The Scarlet Letter,* which Virginia-Ruth had told me about. I knew this was only the beginning of my shame.

"Stained," the woman said again, and closed her eyes.

We stayed that way for three verses of "The Old Rugged Cross." Then the saved-and-sanctified lady opened her eyes, and her features seemed to adjust themselves, as if she had just remembered the key to sanity. She looked very tired. She touched my dress again and nodded and said, "It'll come out. Work a stain like that with shampoo and cold water."

She was talking about my dress. I stood before her, mouth open, while relief banged into me so hard, I wondered if I'd finally been hit by grace. I watched the woman who might once have been as beautiful as my sister said, as beautiful as my sister was herself, and as sane and maybe even as sassy, and then I couldn't seem to get enough air. I breathed hard and wondered what had really happened to her, wondered at all the things that were and were not possible.

I had craned my neck around, trying to see the back of my dress, when big Mrs. Watts bustled in. She smiled grimly at me, and I backed myself against the wall and watched as she wiped the woman's face with paper towels.

"I think she's better now," I said.

But the saved-and-sanctified lady's head looked suddenly too big for her neck, tipping to the side like a heavy, wilting sunflower on a stem.

"Wouldn't you like to lie down somewhere?" Mrs. Watts asked her. "Wouldn't that be a nice thing?" She put her hands under the woman's arms and lifted her to her feet, murmuring comforting nonsense as she led her out of the bathroom.

Then Virginia-Ruth was there. She took in the plastic cup, the folding chair. "What's going on?" she asked. "Mom said to see if you were okay."

I turned away from her and pulled the back of the dress straight. "Is there something on the back of my dress?"

"Yes" she said, making a face. "On *my* dress. It's your period."

I ducked into a stall and sat down, bunching the dress around my waist. Virginia-Ruth peered at me through the crack where the stall door met the frame. "So what happened down there? What did the saved-and-sanctified lady say?"

"What she always says. She was getting upset."

"I saw you come down to the altar," Virginia-Ruth said. She'd tilted her head so that all I could see of her face through the crack was her eyes, and her voice buzzed, a little, against the metal door. "So?"

"What?" I said.

"So, what were you doing down there?"

"I don't know," I said. "It just happened."

Virginia-Ruth stared at me, unblinking, and I felt it even after I closed my eyes and leaned my head against the wall behind the toilet.

"I *see*," Virginia-Ruth said.

I kept my eyes closed until I heard her move.

"I guess you need clean panties," she said, from over by the door.

When she left, I removed her dress and hung it over the top of the stall. The spot was small. I sat down again on the toilet to wait. The singing in the tabernacle was growing very slow and deep, muffled through the walls. You could feel the vibrations under your feet when the congregation hit the next note in unison. Between pauses in the verses and in Reverend Hanson's words, you could just hear people at the altar weeping. The women made soft, short wails, and the men huffed out stiff, reluctant sobs.

I felt like something had been pulled out from under me, like I'd been leaning against the side of a car that had moved, or like someone had come up behind me and nudged the back of my knees to make them buckle. Then I was crying along with everyone else, and suddenly all I wanted was to cry myself to sleep, sitting right there on the tabernacle toilet.

Virginia-Ruth returned and shut the door behind her. "Here," she said, and shoved supplies and a clean pair of underwear under the stall door.

When I stepped out of the stall in my underwear, Virginia-Ruth was applying lipstick in front of the mirror the way she always did, tracing her mouth slowly while moving her face from side to side, as if nothing in life felt as good as that waxy pressure.

"I'm sorry about your dress," I said. I'd wiped my eyes but in the mirror they looked red and puffy.

Virginia-Ruth blotted the lipstick and admired the mouth-shaped O she made on the paper towel. "Well, it's nothing to cry about," she said, frowning at me. "It's going to be an endless altar call, and I get to spend it in the bathroom. I must have done something right." She yanked more paper towels from the dispenser. "None can predict," she added, imitating our father's preaching rhythm, "what motivates the hand of God."

Of this I had never been so sure. I splashed my face while Virginia-Ruth worked at the stain with cold water and soap. We draped the dress over the folding chair to dry and Virginia-Ruth wedged shut the bathroom door with more paper towels, raised the window that looked out over the back field, and withdrew a cigarette from beneath her bra strap. "Care to partake?" she said, lighting the cigarette and offering it to me. I watched my hand reach for it in slow motion, felt it on my lips, and before I exhaled, I moved to stand with my sister at the window.

The Beachcomber

SEE THE MOON?" Reagan said, pointing to where the moon hung large and low, bruised and glowing, over the Atlantic Ocean. "It's cold and dead. *Dead.*"

Laetitia, who sat propped against the roof's ventilation pipe, had been looking at the moon all evening. Now she looked, dutifully, again.

"See those stars?" Reagan pointed straight up over her head.

"Cassiopeia?"

"Any of them," Reagan said. "They're not even *there* anymore." Reagan flattened her voice like what she was saying was very, very important, like the information hadn't been revealed to both of them, months earlier, as they sat next to each other in tenth-grade science. "Nothing matters," Reagan said, squatting in front of Laetitia. Her long, straight blond hair glowed silver; the ends brushed Laetitia's dimpled, sunburned knees and gave them a chill. "Do you get it? Nothing."

"Nothing," Laetitia repeated. "I get it." In some moods

she and Reagan liked to be sarcastic and call each other "bitch," and if they had been in one of these moods Laetitia might have said, "No, do you think you could say it *one more time?*" But tonight Reagan's parents, the Drakes, had introduced them to oysters on the half shell. Oysters made the Drakes amorous, Reagan philosophical, and Laetitia quiet and a little queasy.

Three stories below, on the beach, the receding waves made shining scallop shapes on the sand. In the condominium directly beneath them, Reagan's parents were probably screwing. Reagan said they screwed often, if not spontaneously, on vacation, which was why they always asked her if she wanted to bring a friend. On the far side of the roof, sounds from the street blended together like the buzz of a small city. The two-mile stretch of shoreline highway—the strip—was clogged each night with cruising teenagers on spring break. They hopped in and out of cars that crawled past condos, hotels, and beach retail. They blasted music and got wasted. Earlier that day Reagan said she thought cruising the strip was asinine, and Laetitia, impressed with her use of the word, agreed.

At Laetitia's feet, Reagan collapsed on her back. Her nylon shorts ballooned around her hips. She straightened one leg into the air, regarded it, then dropped it and straightened the other. At home in Kentucky, Reagan and Laetitia had been walking aerobically with ankle weights in preparation for this week in Florida, and Laetitia could see the beginnings of muscles above Reagan's knees. Both girls were overweight—*substantial,* Laetitia's mother said, *not about to blow over in a strong wind.* Laetitia was not as heavy as Reagan, but Reagan was taller, and her legs had better shape. And she had a head full of blond hair, for distraction. Laetitia's own hair was reddish brown and curly, kept tight in a small ponytail while she waited for it to grow long. As for her legs, they went straight to her feet, like she had no ankles at all. *Piano legs,* her mother called them. Laetitia had been expecting them to change with her hips and chest, to curve in at the ankles and knees and out at the calves, but apparently they weren't going to. Now she looked at her legs and remembered.

"I had that dream again," she said to Reagan.

"The wheelchair man?"

"Yeah," Laetitia said, "but this time it's Christmas. I'm carrying a covered dish into a house full of people, and a man takes my coat and a woman takes the dish into the kitchen. I think it's potatoes. Then I figure out that the woman and the man are my husband's parents, and then I'm looking around for my husband, but it's just all these people in their good clothes. The women are wearing jumpers, you know, like teachers, and the men are laughing and punching each other's arms."

"So you see yourself in a house full of people," Reagan said. "I predict that will come true, for you and for everyone else. Big deal."

"Okay," said Laetitia, "but then I go into this hallway where the bedrooms are, and the wheelchair man comes through the door at the end of it. This time his body's normal size, but his legs and arms are shriveled and flat, and he's speaking but he can't get his tongue all the way in his mouth."

"Like Larry Flynt," said Reagan.

"Except he can only say one word and it's my name—*Lathitha*—and his mother hugs me and tells me I'm the only thing he lives for and I can't ever remember seeing him before or deciding to marry him. I'm thinking I should feel bad for him because he's handicapped, and that maybe I should pretend that he's not handicapped, to be nice, but then he's talking inside my head. I try not to hear him, but I still can, and when I close my eyes I can see him through my eyelids. He tells me—" Laetitia began, then stopped.

"What?"

"He tells me he's got a cucumber in his pants for me and there's nothing I can do about it." As Laetitia said "cucumber" out loud, she started to smile. She couldn't help it. It was a scary dream, but saying "cucumber" to Reagan made her laugh. Reagan giggled, too, and then they screamed and pounded their tennis shoes on the roof of the condominium.

"I'm going to pee my pants," Reagan said.

"Cucumber," Laetitia said again, and they laughed some more. One of the reasons Laetitia stayed friends with Reagan, despite her mother's reservations, was that when they were getting along, Reagan made her feel interesting. Laetitia lay back on the roof and stared at the stars, which seemed to throb as she kept herself from blinking, as if her heart were beating in her eyeballs. She and Reagan had been telling each other things they told no one else since junior high. Reagan told Laetitia how she wished her body was a cake of Ivory soap she could carve into shape with a paring knife. Laetitia confessed her love for their French teacher, with his nicotine-stained fingers and red-rimmed eyes that had brimmed over, once, as he reenacted a whole scene from *Casablanca* for the class, singing "The Marseillaise" with such gusto that he spit—a little bit—on the first row.

"Don't worry," Reagan said now. "You're going to marry Monsieur DeMoulin. *L'amour.*"

EACH MORNING, Mrs. Drake woke Reagan and Laetitia at seven for a brisk walk on the beach. Mrs. Drake had damp brown eyes, skin the texture of an orange peel, and a figure that bulged, if lumpily, in all the right places. The things that came out of her mouth astonished Laetitia. Mrs. Drake revealed, for example, that two of her mother's cousins had married each other and produced five eyeless children. ("You'd think they would have stopped after the second," Mrs. Drake said, and Laetitia agreed.) Mrs. Drake described how the eyeless cousins would reach for her when she visited, how they would cry, "Cousin Vonda, come closer."

"Sometimes she lies," said Reagan, but Mrs. Drake ignored her.

Another day Mrs. Drake spooned out her marital history, beginning with how her first husband left her to become a missionary and concluding with Mr. Drake's affair of the year before. Reagan had told Laetitia this already, and about her mother's own affair, too. But Mrs. Drake explained that her affair had accomplished a purpose: to force Mr. Drake into experiencing a like betrayal. They'd "come clean" to Reagan on a trip to the West Coast. Then they chose significant items—a cigarette lighter, a stolen fork—to fling from the rim of the Grand Canyon in a ceremony of letting go. Reagan threw her baby ring, which she had been wearing on a chain around her neck. This made both her parents cry.

"Marriage is hard work," said Vonda Drake, puffing along on the sand. "When two people get married, each of them gives up a little part of themselves to the new whole."

"Which part?" asked Laetitia, looking back at Reagan to see if she'd missed something. Reagan was pumping her arms to burn calories and staring hard into the ocean like she was trying to count waves.

Mrs. Drake said she guessed it was a different part for each person.

On the beach, Reagan and Laetitia covered their bikinis with long T-shirts until they got to their lying-out spot. Both wanted tan stomachs, but neither wanted the exposure before it was absolutely necessary. Reagan's bikini was turquoise, and Laetitia's was purple with pink flowers and a little skirt. She'd bought the suit at the end of nutrition camp last summer, after losing twenty pounds. Now it was tight.

They arranged themselves on the sand between ten and two o'clock, when the sun was most intense. Reagan's system was to turn every half-hour, like a roasting chicken, and Laetitia's system was to lie on one side one day and the other side the next.

Afterward they showered and gave each other the jump test in their bras and panties. "You first," said Reagan, in the Drakes' bedroom, and Laetitia jumped, landing hard on her heels. "Here," said Reagan, touching Laetitia's upper arms, "but not much." Then Reagan touched Laetitia's stomach—"and here"—which always made Laetitia flinch. "And your thighs, of course. A tan makes you thinner, though."

Then Reagan jumped and Laetitia watched to see which parts jiggled the most. "Stomach," she said, "and cheeks. And boobs, but that's good, right? And your thighs are a lot better. Mostly on the inside, there. You look thinner tan, too." It was acceptable to talk about losing weight, to discuss problem areas, but they generally steered clear of words like "fat."

They had decided to buy rings to commemorate the vacation, and in the afternoons they stepped back out into the heat to comb the stores along the strip. The rings would have to be big enough to fit their index, middle, and ring fingers, and of designs you couldn't find at home. Both girls agreed that silver looked better with a tan than gold.

For dinner, the Drakes always took them to Ephraim's Bounty across the street, where Laetitia tried, persistently, to contribute the fifty-dollar bill from her mother. But each night Mr. Drake said, "Your money's no good here," and Mrs. Drake whispered, "We're just glad Reagan has you for a friend," as if Reagan wasn't sitting right there at the table, picking the tails off her shrimp poppers like she couldn't hear and didn't care.

SUNDAY, MONDAY, Tuesday, Wednesday. Laetitia and Reagan bickered through small fights and got over them. By day, they worked on their tans. By night, they headed to the roof with a half gallon of ice cream and two spoons to observe the skinny girls down below, who danced in parking lots, or found themselves pressed up against buildings by beefy boys, or who got so drunk that they threw up in midsentence. Both Laetitia and Reagan agreed that the boys below were at least as pitiful as the boys at home.

Thursday afternoon, on the beach, Laetitia woke from a nap to hear Reagan talking to someone. A boy. Laetitia kept her eyes closed, but she could tell from Reagan's voice—the way it held itself—that she was sucking in her stomach.

"Yeah, we cruise," Reagan said. "The strip, you know. Last night got pretty wild."

"You have wheels, then," said the boy.

"Not exactly."

Laetitia lay facedown. Through the blanket the sand pressed damp and lumpy against her stomach and breasts.

"My brother has a Camaro," said the boy, "but my parents get to drive it while we're down here. We get my dad's truck."

"My dad won't get anything cool because if I'm in a wreck he wants me to be in something big," Reagan said. "He's going to buy me a tank when I get my license. Down here we just ride with guys we meet. Last night we rode in this cool convertible."

"Was it a Mustang?"

Reagan yawned. "I don't really pay attention to make and model, Bobby. It was blue, and it was cool. That's all I know."

Bobby was silent. Then he said, "That your sister?"

"That's Laetitia," Reagan said. "She's my best friend, but she has a drinking problem. It's sad. Last night she almost yakked all over the convertible. I dragged her out here to sleep it off."

Laetitia opened her eyes. The boy was tan and skinny, with a prominent rib cage and a film of downy hair on his legs. He looked like he could still be in junior high. Reagan shrugged into her T-shirt. Her hair seemed blonder, almost white, from the sun. She flipped it over her shoulders.

"Hey, Laetitia," said Bobby, "you got shitfaced."

"I don't want to talk about it," Laetitia said. She tried to sound hung over. She closed her eyes again and listened to them talk about meeting up, maybe, cruising together, maybe, Reagan saying she'd have to see because the guys from last night had pretty much made them say they'd go with them again. But, she said, the vote was still out.

"There's no way he believed that stuff," Laetitia said after Bobby walked away.

"Sure he did," said Reagan.

Later that afternoon, as they headed down the strip to a store called The Beachcomber, Reagan said, "You have to admit, Bobby's cuter than Monsieur DeMoulin."

"No way," said Laetitia.

"Monsieur DeMoulin is going bald," said Reagan.

Laetitia scuffed her sandals against the cement and tried to think of what to say back. "I happen to adore balding men," she said, too long after Reagan had spoken.

Reagan sometimes said things just to irritate Laetitia, and at these times, Laetitia tried not to engage. Her mother said she admired Reagan's quick retort, but thought Laetitia's strengths of stepping back and assessing the big picture before she spoke would serve her better in the long run.

Still damp from her shower, Laetitia was already sweating. Reagan's taupe eye shadow had gummed into the creases of her lids, but Laetitia decided not to tell her.

Two racks of Hawaiian print shirts flanked the entrance of The Beachcomber. Inside, Laetitia inspected the thin silver rings in the ten-dollars-and-under tray. She was almost out of her spending money, and would be obliged to return the fifty-dollar bill to her mother if the Drakes refused it to the very end. The inexpensive rings were so thin that she accidentally bent one, just trying it on, and had to sneak it back into its slot before the woman behind the counter noticed.

Reagan shopped mostly on her father's credit card, so she checked out the silver nugget rings, silver coin rings, rings made of linked dolphins or elephants, plain bands thick as industrial washers, and rings with secret compartments designed, said the cashier woman, to hold poison powder in case you ever wanted to poison someone.

Reagan wiggled her fingers in and out of ring after ring. Laetitia wanted the poison-compartment Indian-head ring the moment she saw it. The front of the ring was a warrior's face, with sunken cheeks and a hooked nose, and the feathered headdress wrapped around your finger. The Indian's left ear was a tiny hinge; his right ear was a tiny latch. It looked like the kind of ring Cher would have worn as the biker-chick mother in *Mask*. Ever since Laetitia had seen the movie with her father, who owned a Harley Sportster 883, she had fantasized about being a biker chick, about getting into fights and having huge, shaggy-headed men ready to beat up other huge men for insulting her. Some days she still thought about being an attorney, though, which would call for the gold jewelry that was coming to her from her grandmother as soon as Laetitia's mother thought she was old enough to appreciate it. Sometimes she tried to imagine a future in which she could be both a biker chick and an attorney, maybe an attorney for bikers, since they always seemed to be in trouble with the law. She would wear her gold jewelry to court, but to meet with the bikers she would wear the massive, heavy silver Indian-head ring. Perhaps as she won cases, the bikers would give her more biker jewelry to show their appreciation.

"What do you think?" asked Reagan, holding out her left hand. On the middle finger, the Indian-head ring bulged as large as a large gumball.

"How much is it?" said Laetitia.

"Fifty," said the saleswoman. Under her short, bleached hair, she waggled her eyebrows as if she, herself, would love to have the Indian-head ring.

"Does it make my finger look big?" Reagan held up her

middle finger. Laetitia could tell she really wanted to know, because she didn't take the opportunity to flip the bird.

"Nooo," said Laetitia. She tried to sound like she was trying not to hesitate. "Well, hold your hand upside down. No, it looks really good."

Reagan pulled off the ring and held it out to Laetitia. "See how heavy it is?"

Laetitia hefted the ring in her palm. "Heavy."

"Try it on," Reagan said.

Laetitia slipped the ring on her index finger. It felt cool and smooth. She popped open the Indian's face, poked the tip of her little finger into the inside of his head, then latched it closed at the ear. Laetitia's fingers were thickish, baggy around the knuckles, but the ring made them look longer and more slender.

"Here," Reagan said, holding out her hand for the ring. Laetitia gave it back. "What would you put in it?" she said, trying it on each of her fingers. "Besides poison, I mean."

"Anything tiny," said the blond woman. "Aspirin, you know, if you're going dancing and don't want to carry a bag. A birth-control pill if you think you might stay over somewhere."

"I don't know," said Reagan. "I really like it, though." She turned toward Laetitia. "Do you think Bobby will like it?"

"Boyfriend?" asked the woman, and Reagan nodded.

"Bobby?" said Laetitia.

"He might even buy it for me," Reagan said.

"Bobby from the beach?" said Laetitia.

"We just met, actually," Reagan said to the woman.

"Love at first sight," the woman said.

"Very first sight," said Laetitia. Reagan smiled at her blandly. Laetitia looked at the Indian head ring. She fingered the fifty in her pocket. "Do you have another one?"

The woman shook her head. "It's the last one," she said, "and I only had three to begin with. They went fast."

"We wouldn't want matching rings, anyway, Laetitia," said Reagan. "And I'm pretty sure I want it. I'm pretty sure Bobby will want me to have it."

"Why don't I hold it for you while you think about it?" said the woman. "You can talk it over with Bobby."

"Do you really want Bobby for a boyfriend?" asked Laetitia as they headed back down the strip to the condo.

"I could do worse," Reagan said. "Monsieur DeMoulin, for example."

"Don't you think he looks like he could be in junior high?" asked Laetitia. "Bobby, I mean."

"Not really," Reagan said. "But he wouldn't be my boyfriend anyway. I could use him to get experience, so that when a viable candidate comes along I'll be ready. See?"

"I guess." Laetitia looked down at her bare hands, remembering the weight of the Indian-head ring.

"I could get lucky down here in Florida," Reagan said. "I like what that woman said about keeping a birth-control pill in that ring. I should probably start thinking about protection."

"You mean sex?" said Laetitia.

"What do you think 'lucky' means?"

Laetitia pondered this. "I mean, shouldn't you be able to use a tampon first?"

"I can use a tampon anytime I want to," Reagan snapped. "I just don't want to. Ever heard of toxic shock syndrome?"

Laetitia didn't answer. She'd been at the Drakes' during the last tampon attempt, when Reagan had emerged from the bathroom red-faced, fuming that it hadn't worked and she didn't want to talk about it.

"What does your mother use for birth control when Mr. Hawkins stays over?" Reagan asked.

"He doesn't stay over."

"Of course he does," Reagan said. "He just leaves before you wake up."

Laetitia tried to picture Mr. Hawkins, Evan, tiptoeing out of her mother's bedroom clutching his shoes. He was a slight, handsome band teacher, who had played his sousaphone for Laetitia's fifteenth birthday. Laetitia's mother had seen Mr. Hawkins, Evan, on Saturday nights since her divorce a year ago. She described him to Laetitia as old-fashioned and companionable. "I told you," Laetitia said. "I think he's gay."

"Really?" Reagan frowned as if hearing this for the first time. "Well, then, your mother must be a fag hag."

"She is not," said Laetitia.

"Don't be sensitive, Laetitia. Fag hags can't help that fags appreciate them."

"What if I said your mother was a fag hag?" Laetitia said, a question that seemed inadequate somehow.

"Well if it was true then why would I care? Anyway, my mother's tubes are tied. She doesn't need birth control. Do you know what a diaphragm is? It's a ring that goes around your cervix. Your cervix size is your true ring size, and if you get caught without your diaphragm, you can put a regular ring around your cervix and it will work the same way. Keep that in mind when looking for rings."

"You're making that up," said Laetitia.

"Oh, right," said Reagan. "I forget you're the one who knows. You got felt up at fat camp."

"Nutrition camp." Laetitia's face flushed. She'd made up a story about a boy there. "Has anyone ever told you you're antagonistic?" she said. "Do you even know what 'antagonistic' means?"

"Bitch," Reagan said, narrowing her eyes.

"Bitch," Laetitia said back.

They were mad for a moment, and tried to stare each other down, but when Reagan stopped in front of another store and asked, "How's my makeup?" Laetitia said, "Close your eyes," licked her finger and fixed the eye-shadow problem.

At night, headlights and taillights turned the strip into a red-and-white slow-moving snake. Signs lit up the palm trees from below, bright against the dark sky, obliterating the stars. Kids on foot weaved in and out of the cars or walked beside the road, and Reagan and Laetitia found themselves behind two darkly tanned girls who still wore their string bikinis. Barefoot, the thin girls swung their legs from the hip, lanky and effortless. Laetitia could feel the inside seams of her jeans shorts rubbing against each other. She untucked her T-shirt and let it hang wrinkled past her hips.

Reagan wore blue soccer shorts and a huge gray sweatshirt. For the first time, Laetitia saw what her mother meant when she said that Reagan carried her weight well. She moved fluidly, at least, like her arms and legs belonged to her, while Laetitia lumbered along beside her, feeling like walking was something she had to remember how to do.

The girls in front of them carried clear plastic cups of beer. When boys called from the cars, these girls lifted their hands carelessly and smirked at each other. Soon a white convertible pulled over and they draped themselves over the backseat and were gone.

"We could go look at rings," Laetitia suggested as they approached The Beachcomber, but Reagan wasn't talking, suddenly, and they passed the store in silence. A hundred feet farther on, four or five kids sat at several round tables outside a soda shop. "We could get a Coke," Laetitia said, and Reagan ignored her. They passed the soda shop. They passed a store where you could have a photograph superimposed on a T-shirt and a recording studio where you could make a tape of yourself singing a song to canned music. At the next sandwich place, Reagan turned and walked toward the entrance without consulting or even looking at Laetitia. She ordered a large cheese fries and two Diet Cokes while Laetitia stood dumbly at her side. When Laetitia followed her to a table outdoors, Reagan said, "He's from Macon County, Alabama," as if they'd been chatting about Bobby all evening. "He's fifteen and he plays soccer. We could visit each other over summer vacation."

"So you do want him for a boyfriend," said Laetitia.

"I'm speculating, Laetitia, that's all. But I do have a feeling. Sometimes you just know." Regan spoke loudly, like she was in a play and her voice had to reach the back of the theater, like she thought everyone around them was listening. When someone from a passing car called, "Hey, baby," Reagan smiled as if she knew it was meant for her.

A large blue truck crawled by, three boys and two girls in the back, and Reagan jumped to her feet so fast her chair tipped over. "Is that Bobby?" She lifted her hand to her eyes, an exaggerated shield against the headlights. "He better not be with another girl." She righted her chair, still staring at the truck.

"He's not," said Laetitia as the truck rolled past. "It's not him."

"Not if he knows what's good for him," Regan said, running a hand through her straight pale hair. She sat back down to her fries. Laetitia nursed her Diet Coke. She found she did not have an appetite.

"Where did you say he was going to be?"

"We didn't make it definite," Reagan said. "Neither of us wants to be tied down." Reagan squinted up the strip. In the distance, a huge pink pelican lit up the sky.

"If you see him again, maybe you should make it definite," Laetitia said.

Reagan polished off the last cheese fry and frowned at Laetitia. "You didn't eat anything."

"Is there a law against that?"

Regan blinked at her, once, twice, then rose and stalked to the garbage can and threw away her trash. She stalked to the sidewalk and began stalking back in the direction of the condo.

"What about Bobby?" Laetitia asked when she caught up.

"Bobby doesn't know what he's missing," said Reagan.

FRIDAY IT RAINED. Laetitia began a letter to her mother that described the rainy sky over the rainy ocean, with the gulls, between showers, bright white against the gray. She didn't want to tell her mother she and Reagan weren't getting along. Sometimes Laetitia's mother took her side too fervently, and then Laetitia found herself having to talk her mother into allowing her to spend time with Reagan again when things got better. The Drakes declared it family day, and stayed in. "You need to give all those boys a break," said Mr. Drake as they played Clue.

"Oh, Daddy," Reagan said, but she gave Laetitia a meaningful glance. Reagan had been extra nice this morning, even putting away the sofa bed herself and letting Laetitia go first in the bathroom. While Mrs. Drake made lunch, Reagan announced she was going to The Beachcomber to buy the Indian-head ring, and Laetitia took a walk on the beach in the rain, by herself, following the shifting line the water left on the sand. The gray sea, frothy with rain, looked like how her stomach felt sometimes around Reagan. One moment they could be best friends, and the next Reagan seemed to find Laetitia intolerable, leaving her flailing around for the right words to switch things back.

Laetitia had no appetite for the leftover sandwiches and salad Mrs. Drake fixed for lunch. At dinner she couldn't finish her fried shrimp. She wasn't trying to leave food, like they'd suggested at camp; she just wasn't hungry.

Reagan elbowed her. "Are you trying not to eat, or what?"

"No," said Laetitia. As Mr. and Mrs. Drake enjoyed their second drinks, Reagan began to sneak shrimp off Laetitia's plate. The Indian-head ring was even larger and more silver than Laetitia had remembered. Laetitia pushed her plate toward Reagan. "Go ahead," she said.

"No, thanks," said Reagan, "I'm not really that hungry," but she continued to eat Laetitia's shrimp until they were gone.

SATURDAY WAS SUNNY again. On the beach, Laetitia read one of Mrs. Drake's very thick novels, in which the heroine and her ex-husband were saying things *acidly* to each other, which was a sure sign they would be getting back together. Laetitia had eaten only toast for breakfast. By noon she did not feel hungry, exactly, merely aware of a mild ache in her gut, an airless sucking from the inside. She was interested in the feeling, and wondered how long she could keep it up.

At two, Reagan was asleep, or pretending to be. Laetitia walked down to the water without first putting on her T-shirt. Her skin had turned a deep brown, and she thought she might look thinner. She felt thinner. She walked right past all the people and into the water, and then she swam a ways down the beach, wishing she'd started doing this before vacation was almost over. She loved submerging herself just under the water's surface, loved when a wave buoyed her up and let her back down as if she were supple as a fish. Afterwards she found Reagan sitting up and talking to Bobby, who stood over her. As they both turned to watch Laetitia's approach, Laetitia wished she'd worn her shirt. Reagan smiled with all her teeth.

Laetitia reached them and picked up her book. "I'm going inside," she said.

"You what?" Reagan said. "Why?" But Laetitia was already on her way.

Inside the condo, she finished the letter to her mother:

I met a boy. His name is Bobby, and he's from Macon, Alabama. He is boring, but nice. I am more tan than I have ever been, and I have lost some weight from swimming in the ocean. There are not as many shells as I thought there would be, so I haven't really collected any for you. I will see you soon. Probably before you even get this. Love, Laetitia.

She addressed it, then turned out the light and sat on the floor. The condominium was cool and dark, all the blinds pulled, fake snake plant rustling in the corner beside the air-conditioning vent. Laetitia felt the empty stomach pain, again, and noticed that with it came waves of peace; the furniture's dim outlines grew sharper, and smells began to separate from each other. Mr. Drake's Jack Daniel's; Mrs. Drake's perfume (Charlie!); coconut suntan oil; nail polish remover; the tangy, almost fruity smell of whatever they used to clean the carpets. Laetitia breathed it in and wondered if this was what it felt like to be an adult. Parentless among people who weren't necessarily on your side. Sitting in the dark, knowing all the smells.

The sun came in the open door with Reagan, who also opened the blinds then headed to the freezer and pulled out a pint of ice cream. "Just sitting in the dark," she said to Laetitia, handing her a spoon. "Weird." Laetitia dug out a small spoonful and licked at it. Pralines and cream. The light in her eyes and the cold in her mouth made her head hurt. On the couch, Reagan ate quickly and neatly. The Indian-head ring bobbed in and out of the carton, and Reagan saw her looking. "Don't you love it?" she said. "You can wear it sometimes. I mean after I wear it for a while, and not to school, of course. I'll be wearing it to school. But other times, maybe."

"Thanks."

"Here." Reagan offered her the ice cream again.

Laetitia shook her head.

"What are you, starving yourself?"

"No." Laetitia watched as Reagan kept eating. It wasn't that the ice cream didn't taste good, and it wasn't that she wasn't hungry, because now she was. She simply didn't want any, and when she tried to want some, just to see if she could, she couldn't. Reagan made her way through the carton. It seemed to Laetitia, now, that the less she ate, the more Reagan wanted to, in direct proportion. She wondered if this could be true.

"I've been thinking about what you said," said Reagan, scraping the bottom of the carton. "You said that next time I saw Bobby, we should set a time and a place to meet instead of maybe just running into each other. That's what we did this time."

"I don't think that's exactly original advice." The feeling in Laetitia's stomach made even her voice sound different. Older and ironic. She liked how she'd thought of the words "original advice."

"Oh, I know," said Reagan, her hands now still, holding the spoon and empty carton. "I just thought you'd like to know that we have a specific time and place to meet him tonight."

"We?"

"You have to come with me," Reagan said. "I need you."

Laetitia licked her spoon and looked wistfully into the empty ice-cream carton. "All right," she said. The hungry feeling was becoming less peaceful and more hungry.

Reagan tipped the carton toward her. "Change your mind? All gone. Sorry."

Laetitia got up and went to the kitchen and opened the fridge. Nothing but two carrots and a cucumber. Laetitia rinsed a carrot under the faucet and munched on it. She held up the cucumber. "What does this make you think of?" she asked Reagan.

"Lathitha," Reagan said, her tongue lolling. "Lathitha, come to me."

OUTSIDE The Beachcomber, Bobby's older brother, Scott, collected money for beer. Laetitia gave him her last five-dollar bill, and Reagan slipped him a bill, too—more than a five, because Scott said, "Baby," and kissed the air near her cheek. Reagan looked like she was trying to kiss the air, too, but got him squarely on the jaw instead. "Watch out, Bob," said Scott. Then he crossed the street to find the man who bought for them.

Besides Bobby and Scott and Ray, their ten-year-old brother, there were two dark-haired girls and another boy. Everyone went around and said their names, but Laetitia could remember only Stacia, and she forgot which dark-haired girl Stacia was. She clambered into the truck bed after Reagan, Bobby, and Ray, while the others crowded into the truck cab. When Scott returned, he set a case of beer in the back and took two flat bottles up front. He rapped the back window and said, "Be good back there," before pulling into the slow line of cars.

Right away, Ray started talking about the glass-bottomed boat he'd been on that day. He was young enough that Laetitia felt like she was babysitting, which she almost didn't mind. Above the water, Ray had watched a man haul in a small shark with a net. Beneath the water he'd seen a school of anchovies that glimmered silver and looked like the sky.

"Shut up about the boat, Ray," said Bobby.

Reagan and Bobby slouched up against the wheel hub, Bobby's arm around her. Ray passed around cans of beer.

"I hate beer," Laetitia told Ray. She'd tasted it from her dad's cans.

"I do, too," Ray said, "but I'm thirsty."

"I love beer," Reagan said, and slurped from the can. Bobby stroked Reagan's bare arm, where her T-shirt sleeve ended, while he stared into his beer can like he didn't know what his hand was doing.

In the truck cab, one of the girls was sitting on the other boy's lap with her shirt off, her breasts glowing white and red and green in the lights from the strip. Laetitia could see both dark nipples, and then one breast was covered by the back of the boy's head. Ray was watching, too, and it was embarrassing that they were both seeing a thing like that at the same time. Laetitia tried another sip of beer. It was still bitter in her mouth, but now there was a sweetness when she swallowed. It made her bold. "Are they going to have sex up there, or what?" she asked no one in particular.

Bobby and Reagan both looked toward the cab. "They always stop in time," he said. "We're Catholic."

"So am I," said Reagan, who was Southern Baptist. She crossed herself.

"You have pretty hair," Bobby told her. He didn't seem to care that Laetitia and Ray were right there. Ray settled into the corner of the truck bed with a blanket, right up against the cab. Laetitia nestled into the other corner, with her beer. They were creeping along at ten miles an hour, and when they reached the last neon sign, they turned around and crept back the other way. It was as asinine as it had looked from three stories up. Laetitia tried to conjure Monsieur DeMoulin in his leather jacket, on a motorcycle, her arms wrapped around him as they hurtled dark and loud through the deserted warm Florida night. They'd stop at a beach, and then who knew what would happen? Laetitia always tried to think about Monsieur DeMoulin before she went to sleep so that she would dream about him, but it never worked.

When the truck lurched over to the side of the strip, Laetitia opened her eyes to find Ray asleep and Bobby and Reagan pulling away from each other, as if they'd been kissing. Everyone in the truck cab piled out, the one girl still struggling back into her shirt. Now they wanted the back of the truck.

"Bobby, you're driving," said Scott. He let down the trapdoor. "Out."

"No, I'm not," Bobby said. He stayed put, and so did Reagan. Laetitia scooted out of the truck bed on her bottom and stood in the dirt beside the road.

"You're driving or you're walking," Scott told Bobby. The older girls were already launching themselves into the truck bed, arranging blankets and towels.

"Ray," Scott said.

"Oh, leave him," said one of the girls. "He's sound asleep."

"Out," Scott said again to Bobby.

"Pisser," Bobby said as he and Reagan climbed out of

the back. Scott tossed Bobby the keys and climbed in back after the others. Soon the four of them had tangled themselves among the blankets and sleeping bags.

Laetitia started to move around to the passenger side of the truck, when Reagan said, "Laetitia can drive."

"No," said Laetitia, "I can't."

"You're sixteen," Reagan reminded her. "You have your license."

"I'm fifteen, and I have a permit."

"So you know how," said Bobby.

"Her dad taught her," said Reagan.

Laetitia glanced into the truck cab. "This is a stick shift," she said. "I only had one lesson on a stick shift."

"You can do it," Bobby said supportively. "Come on. No one goes over twenty, anyway."

"You drive," Laetitia said to Bobby. "Or you," she said to Reagan.

Bobby and Reagan exchanged glances. "Bobby and I have other things in mind," Reagan said.

Bobby drained his beer and tossed the can by the side of the road. "I can't drive," he said. "I've had three beers. You wouldn't want me to drive drunk, would you?"

"Get the fucking show on the road!" Scott yelled from the back.

Bobby attempted to put one foot in front of the other, and toppled to his knees, laughing. "See?" he said. "I couldn't pass a sobriety test."

Laetitia took the keys. She gave Reagan a murderous look, but Reagan was already maneuvering herself into the passenger side. Laetitia adjusted the driver's seat as far forward as it would go, and could just barely reach the pedals. Then she found the knob for the headlights and started the engine, remembering to push in the clutch first. She flicked on her left blinker, and when another truck stopped to let her into the stream of cars, she tried to ease off the clutch and apply the gas, but the truck stalled with a yanking that Laetitia felt in all her internal organs.

"Jesus Mary," shouted one of the boys from the back. A foot thumped against the metal of the truck bed and Scott's face appeared at the back window. Laetitia pumped in the clutch and tried again, and this time the truck roared out into the line of cars.

She was okay if traffic did not stop. That way she could keep the truck rolling forward in first or second, with a good distance between the truck—her truck—and the truck ahead of her. Second gear was better, though it meant she had to brake and push in the clutch and downshift to first when things slowed, or the truck started to whine. She gripped the wheel tightly, gritted her teeth, and amazingly, as they progressed down the strip, she began to get the hang of it. They'd traveled only one mile in fifteen minutes, but Laetitia was getting used to idling and coasting, easing from a full stop into first. In fact, driving the truck was the most fun thing about this whole vacation since Reagan met Bobby.

She'd almost forgotten about them in the seat beside her. She'd also tuned out the noise of the strip and the truck radio that played a station featuring requests only from kids who were on spring break. When traffic stopped again, she pushed in the clutch and saw that Bobby was kneeling on the middle of the seat, leaning over Reagan with his back to the road. They were kissing with great concentration. Laetitia could hear the wet clicking of tongues, and in the half dark she could see one of Bobby's hands on Reagan's leg, and the other disappearing under her shirt.

The truck ahead started moving again. It was an old model, yellow with tiny round red taillights like evil eyes. Laetitia worked the gas and clutch. The magic point where the gear engaged seemed a natural thing, always there and waiting to be rediscovered. The figures in the truck bed had flattened out of her rearview. In a convertible behind her, a girl sat up on the trunk with her feet in the backseat, dancing with the top part of her body.

Now Bobby was kissing Reagan's neck. The neon sign of the Pink Pelican Hotel turned her face pink, and she blinked once at Laetitia then squeezed her eyes tightly shut and giggled.

Laetitia looked back to the road and edged the truck forward like a pro. When Bobby pushed Reagan up against the passenger door, her soccer shorts made slippery sounds against the vinyl seat, and Laetitia locked the electric locks so she wouldn't spill out.

Reagan said, "Oh," and Laetitia looked again. Bobby's hand was up the leg of Reagan's shorts.

"Ow!" Reagan said, and then, "Oh, okay." She sounded as if she were talking on the phone to someone who was giving her bad news. Laetitia looked back to the road and slammed on the brakes to avoid hitting the next truck. The engine stalled.

"Christ," yelled someone in the back.

Laetitia restarted the engine and let it idle. She began to wish very much that she were alone on the dark beach.

"Ow!" said Reagan again, loud.

"What?" Bobby said. "What?"

"Nothing. Sorry." She giggled again.

They slowly approached the Drakes' condominium building on the left, then passed it, nearing the part of the strip where they would have to U-turn again to drive back the other way. Reagan squirmed on the seat, now, breathing painfully through her teeth. Bobby's arm was up her shorts to his elbow.

"What's wrong with you?" Bobby said. He whispered every word but "wrong." He appeared to be jabbing at her with his hand.

"Nothing," Reagan said. "I like it." But she closed her legs the next time he tried to jab her, her thighs making a soft, slapping sound. Laetitia did not know she'd decided to lay on the horn until the sound of it—urgent and wrenching—made her jump. All the passengers yelled at the same time.

Bobby yanked his hand out of Reagan's shorts and turned toward Laetitia. "What the fuck?" Then: "What are you looking at?"

Laetitia's honk had set off a chorus of horns around her. She opened her mouth to say the first thing she thought of, which was that Bobby sounded just like a little kid, but just then the truck banged into the bumper of the truck in front of them, throwing Laetitia against the steering wheel and Bobby and Reagan into the dash. There was a general disruption in the truck bed.

"Hey!" said Bobby.

"Oh my god!" said Reagan.

Scott vaulted out of the truck bed. "What the hell happened?" he shouted at Laetitia, as the other driver opened his own door. Then Scott said quietly, quickly, "Never mind. You and your friend just start walking. You weren't driving, you weren't drinking. Okay? Get a move on."

LAETITIA STOPPED on the sidewalk to wait for Reagan, who was walking so hard she set off the slight, mad, isolated jiggle in her upper cheeks. When she caught up with Laetitia, she passed her without speaking.

"Reagan." Laetitia trotted to stay behind her.

Reagan held her palm over her shoulder. "Do not speak to me."

Laetitia fell back several steps. Here, at the edge of the strip, the night was less noisy, and Laetitia could hear the waves, one after the other, crashing and hissing out onto the sand, and could even see—in the spaces between the buildings—their white foam edges dissolving back to darkness. Ahead of her, Reagan walked faster.

When the truck approached in the line of cars, Bobby was leaning out the passenger side window, leering in a way that gave Laetitia a bad feeling.

Reagan glanced at him, too, and increased her speed.

As the truck passed, Bobby stretched his whole upper body out the window and yelled, "Fat girls need love, too— right, Reagan?"

Laetitia gave him the finger, but Reagan kept walking. Bobby ducked back inside and the truck inched forward until it was finally six or seven cars ahead by the time they reached the condominium.

"Bobby's a real penis," Laetitia said when she caught up with Reagan at the door. Reagan was not crying, but in the light over the door her face looked purple underneath her tan. "Breathe," Laetitia told her.

"You shut up," Reagan said, her voice raspy.

The condominium was empty. The clock on the stove read 10:05, but it felt like the middle of the night. Reagan stomped to the bedroom and slammed the door behind her, locking it. Laetitia slid open the glass door to the balcony and gulped in the ocean air. She was feeling dizzy, and wondered if she should eat something after all.

In the apartment behind her, Reagan wasn't finished stomping around. She stomped out of the bedroom, into the kitchen, and then back to the bedroom. Laetitia stood looking out at the beach, enjoying her dizziness, wondering why it was something people complained about, until she took a step and the patio floor seemed to have risen. She put her head between her legs. When she stood upright again, she felt better. In the apartment, she began folding her clothes into her suitcase. She planned to check on Reagan when she finished. There was the small possibility that Reagan had picked up a knife from the kitchen, though Laetitia doubted Reagan would go that far, even if she was feeling dramatic. When Laetitia folded her jean shorts, she felt in the front pocket for the fifty-dollar bill, but it wasn't there. Laetitia searched all the pockets, then all the pockets of her other shorts, then the rest of her suitcase, then her purse, which was the last place she ever kept money. She got up and knocked on the bedroom door.

"Go away," Reagan said. She was crying, but she had not locked the door again. Laetitia pushed it open and then closed it behind her. Reagan sat on the carpet under the window, in the faint glow from a security light outside. Laetitia sat down on the bed.

"Are you okay?"

"Do I sound okay?" asked Reagan. "You really screwed things up for me tonight, Laetitia."

"With Bobby?" Laetitia said. "You wanted to stay in the truck with Bobby?"

"I don't want to talk about it."

"Even after what he said?" Laetitia said.

"I didn't hear anything," Reagan said.

"You didn't hear anything."

"He didn't say anything," Reagan said. "Is there an echo in here?"

Laetitia sighed. Then she remembered. "Have you seen my money?"

"No."

Laetitia waited to see if Reagan would say more. Sometimes when she lied, she overdid it. Instead, Reagan was making small noises in the back of her throat, little puffs of effort and discomfort. Laetitia stared at her own shadowy reflection in the mirror over the bed. It occurred to her that she might be prettier in the near dark, her features forming an interesting set of shadows.

"My fifty-dollar bill?" she said to Reagan.

"You mean the fifty-dollar bill you were supposed to give my parents?" Reagan said. She made the noises again.

"What are you doing down there?" Laetitia asked.

"None of your goddamned business."

Laetitia peered down to where Reagan sat on the floor, wedged between the bed and the wall. She was sitting with her knees up, her right hand inside the leg of her shorts as Bobby's had been. While Laetitia looked, Reagan withdrew her hand. She was holding the cucumber.

"Reagan," Laetitia said, but her voice seemed to get sucked out of the room with the rest of the sound. When she could hear again, Reagan was sniffling.

"I'm getting it over with, that's all," she said. "It doesn't fucking hurt after the first time."

"That was a *dream* about the cucumber," Laetitia said. "That was not a good dream."

"Ow," Reagan said. "Ow." She breathed out hard through her teeth. "Shit."

Laetitia wouldn't look. "Don't," she said. "You can't just stick that thing inside you."

Reagan pounded the back of her head against the wall so hard that Laetitia felt the vibration travel up through the bed. "No," Reagan said. "I can't stick this fucking thing

inside me because I can't fucking get it *in*. You're so pre-
dictable, Laetitia. I know everything you say before you
even say it."

"No, you don't," said Laetitia.

"See? I knew you would say that." Someone in the next
condo turned on a television.

"You took my money," Laetitia said.

"You're supposed to give it to my family, and I'm part
of my family. You owe me, anyway, after you wrecked
tonight." Reagan motioned with the cucumber. "You still
owe me," she said, "and now you have to pay me back."

Laetitia looked at the cucumber and made herself
laugh—"HA"—like Reagan was obviously joking.

"Someone else has to push it in," said Reagan. "I can't
do it because I stop when it hurts."

"No," said Laetitia. "You can have the money."

"I already have it," Reagan said. "I already spent it. It
was mine to spend, anyway."

"You know what Bobby said, Reagan?" In the next
condo, the television fell quiet. "While we were walking
back on the side of the road, he said, 'Fat girls need love,
too.' Bobby thought you were fat, and so do I." Laetitia
meant to sound as cold and hateful as Reagan had sounded,
but the words got squeezed through her chest and came
out sounding thin.

Reagan answered her, but a buzzing in Laetitia's head
kept her from hearing. "What?"

"I said, 'I'll give you the ring.'" In the shadow, Reagan
held her hands close to her body and struggled to remove

the ring from her middle finger. It was cold and heavy in Laetitia's palm.

"All you have to do is push it in," said Reagan. "I put some Vaseline on it. I'll put it in the right place. All you have to do is push hard one time."

Laetitia looked at the ring. She tried it on her index finger, then her thumb, then her ring finger. It looked and felt exactly the same as it had before, and she waited for the wanting of it to come back. "When we get back to Kentucky," said Laetitia, "I never want to speak to you again." She slipped off the ring and laid it on the bed.

"Are you going to do it, or not?"

Laetitia got to her feet, then knelt in front of Reagan. Regan pressed her back full against the wall, using her left hand to move the cucumber into position. "Here," Reagan said. She found Laetitia's hand and placed it around the end of the cucumber. It was thick and waxy, like the handle of something, and Reagan's soccer shorts lay cool against the top of Laetitia's wrist. She had to bend over Reagan, slightly, for leverage, and with her other hand she braced herself against the wall. Laetitia smelled the smell; she never knew what to call it. "I'm not going to look," she said. "You can't make me look."

"Just get it over with," said Reagan.

It was resistance of a kind Laetitia had never felt. Pushing against something solid and regretful that was nevertheless giving way, the way the inside of a throat might to a fist. Reagan's squeal faded to a whimper of defeat, which sounded to Laetitia both strange and familiar. She let go of the cucumber. She rushed from the bedroom and through the dark, empty living room, over her packed suitcase and out onto the balcony, where she sucked in deep gulps of air. She bent her head back to the sky and let the stars throb into her head until she was dizzy again.

The sliding glass door opened all the way, rumbling in its tracks, but Laetitia kept her head bent back. Reagan stood near, breathing hard. There was the rustle of soccer shorts as Reagan took a step, the slight movement of air from the motion of Reagan's arm. Then Reagan wasn't there anymore, and it was only the waves and the distant sound of the strip and the pinging of the ring far below as it hit the top of the bathhouse and bounced to land silent in the sparse beach grass, or maybe in the sand, where Laetitia might begin to look for it in the morning.

Holy Land

BY TWO O'CLOCK, Alton lies on the couch, the old, television-watching couch that used to be the good couch, listening to back-to-back soap operas through the padded headphones Vi bought him when he retired in the spring. He's seventy, and for the first time in his life he is waiting for nothing to happen. He has always hated the look of retired people. Careful clothes, settled eyes in happy, hobby-induced expressions.

He'd had the TV up so loud, Vi tells Poe, that she could hear every whisper all the way out in the garden. That, and she'd come in and he'd be sleeping through it all anyway.

Vi and Poe are sitting at the kitchen table, sipping iced tea from tall, dark purple metallic cups. It's a hot day, for New Hampshire, and they're damp from dipping in the lake, and their skin is warm and lake-smelling, like frogs or fish, like the sandy bottom muck, and like something else, something clean.

Poe says the headphones are a good thing. She says she doesn't exactly want her daughter, Cricket, hearing all that exaggerated real life—not yet, anyway. Isn't it enough already that the girl has a father who calls himself "the Prophet"?

Vi says something low and disgusted, and Poe laughs her new laugh, smart and disappointed like she's lived through everything once and expects an encore.

Cricket is out on the screened-in porch, lying on her stomach on the built-in bed with the two deep drawers under it for Vi's extra storage. She is reading *Head o' W-Hollow* by Jesse Stuart, who is on the summer list because he is a Kentucky writer and Poe is a Kentucky librarian. Vi is Poe's mother, and Poe is Cricket's mother, and it is a joke in the family that they look like the same person at different stages of very different lives. They all have gray eyes and coarse curly hair that is either charming, on Vi, who wears it short and has a gray streak in front, or difficult-looking, on Poe, who tries all manner of clips and curlers, or so unruly and fuzzy on Cricket that it is always in a ponytail high on her head, or in a tight braid that she doesn't unwind for a week. It's dark hair, often confused with the color black, though Vi, who knows she's not racist because one of her lifelong friends, Patricia, is black, says that only black people, and some Oriental people, have truly black hair.

This year Poe is divorced, so she and Cricket are spending the entire summer with Vi and Alton in the lake house he built from the ground up, where everything smells like paint. Vi and Poe are repainting, pale purple over the current pale yellow. Vi has repainted the inside walls every two years since the house was finished over thirty years ago. Repainting keeps things clean. In some rooms the corners are slightly rounded from layers of paint.

Poe has selected twenty-five books for Cricket to read over the summer. Some, like *To Kill a Mockingbird,* Poe has chosen because she read them as a child and loved them. Some of the other books she hasn't yet had a chance to read. She's trying them out on Cricket before placing them on the library shelves at J. P. Morgan Elementary back home.

You're still young, Vi is saying.

Youngish, says Poe.

You've got a smart figure.

Poe laughs again. Then she calls, hey, to Cricket. The door between the kitchen and porch is propped open with a brick, for the cross draft.

Ma'am? says Cricket, who is nine. Vi insists on ma'am and sir in her house.

How's Jesse Stuart?

Silence. The fan whirs; a police cruiser tracks down the gravel drive to the one-room station in the next lot.

Colloquial, says Cricket.

Colloquial? whispers Vi in the kitchen.

Oh, yes, says Poe, smug.

You're a very smart girl, Vi says, her voice doing what it always does when she talks to Cricket, stretching around the words like she has to try to say words, like she's speaking from something already written down, with directions on how it should be said. Like a play.

Cricket says ummhmm because it's her grandmother and she's old and can't help it that she still talks to Cricket like a baby. And Cricket won't be rude because she's still a born-again Christian, even though her mother isn't anymore.

Like a play, and when Poe and Vi start talking again, Cricket sneaks the tiny paperback script of *The Sound of Music* and hides it, open, in the Jesse Stuart book. She snuck it from the library. She keeps her place in it with a tiny sliver of wood from Jesus' cross that the prophet brought her from the Holy Land. Poe loves *The Sound of Music,* the movie, anyway, and Cricket would of course be allowed to read it, but she wants to keep something she reads just for herself. So she won't have to answer questions about it or share it at all, really. Also, she thinks she might become an actress. Poe is always saying that Cricket is melodramatic, and that her voice carries a mile, but that's not a good thing.

Cricket has iced tea, too. The tall metal cup has a little frost on the outside, so cold it makes her fingers ache and she keeps it down on the floor by the bed, not holding it with one hand the way she does when she drinks from a regular glass. This morning Vi got down a box from the attic and got out these cups and cried a little. They were from the pre-retirement house, the one with enough bedrooms so that Poe didn't have to sleep on the screened-in porch and Cricket didn't have to sleep on the couch. That was before Alton and Vi lived year-round at the lake house.

Then the lake house, just for vacations, seemed more interesting, full of things Cricket had forgotten about—iron skillets, green glass plates with green glass dividers right on them to separate the food, Vi's collection of tiny ceramic birds. Now the lake house is all there is, and that's what it seems like. Boring and knowable.

Outside, the meter man cuts across the yard in his khaki uniform shorts, for the weekly reading. He's sinewy and brown, a fisherman, and he has a way of making people who talk to him feel as though they're using too many words. It's the way he looks at you, Vi says, as if he's hearing you and waiting for you to stop at the same time. Vi always brings him a tall cup of iced tea and he says thank you and she says bring the cup back and he says no need and drinks it down right there and hands it back to her without looking at her. Still, she whispers to Poe in the kitchen, it's important to be nice. When tools started disappearing in Laconia, it took them weeks to figure out it was the meter man. They feel underappreciated, Vi explains.

Cricket watches her grandmother lean out the door to give the meter man the tea. Vi's legs are slim and white and hairless. She shaves in the tub every single afternoon. No veins, either. This is because Vi has never, not once, crossed her legs at the knees. Ankles only, and she pinches whenever Cricket forgets. A woman has to keep up her legs, and it's never too early to start. Vi closes the screen door and makes a face at the meter man's back. She turns to Cricket, squaring her shoulders and putting on a smile like a present, but Cricket is looking at her book again. Then Vi moves to the doorway of the kitchen and squares herself off and smiles again, like another, recently rewrapped present.

Don't you worry she reads too much? she says to Poe.

No.

Soon she'll need glasses.

Maybe.

She should be outside more.

She swam this morning.

She should be outside in the sun.

She's *my* daughter, says Poe.

Silence, then the hollow rinsing of cups.

That meter man knows my name, says Vi, he's just too rude to use it.

ONE OF VI'S LIFELONG friends, Ruby, comes over on a Wednesday and says her son Charlie will be visiting for a week and his divorce is final, too. A dinner is arranged. Charlie and Poe had been in high school together, he more popular than she—he never gave her the time of day when they were in school, Poe says—but she'd been a late blossomer, appreciated by bookish men, older men, in college. Now, Ruby and Vi reason when Poe returns to painting the bedroom, things might very well be different.

Shhh, says Vi when Cricket enters the kitchen for a drink.

Hey there, Cricket, says Ruby. I would like you to know I quit smoking since the last time we chatted. My body is a temple, right?

Cricket nods, chastened, because this year the Lord has

told her not to go around telling people how to live, but instead to witness by example. Since last year Ruby has put on weight like a spider, still skinny in the arms and legs.

She's quite a Christian, says Vi. Vi's eyes crinkle up like she's fond of Cricket.

Not a bad thing to be, says Ruby.

Oh, we're all Christian, says Vi as Cricket leaves the room. There's Christian, then there's Christian. Then she's telling Ruby how Cricket's father came back from Jerusalem thinking he was divine. How he camps on the edge of town in Kentucky and prophesies for the people who visit him, and hasn't bathed in a year, which isn't true. He bathes every week in the basement bathroom of the Baptist church, and sometimes Cricket helps him wash out his clothes.

In the bedroom Poe stands on a chair to get at the wall where it meets the ceiling.

I don't want to be set up, she says, jabbing the brush into the corner, scratching the white ceiling with purple paint. She is working her way around the top of the wall, covering the pale yellow with a fringe of violet brush-strokes. Over her bathing suit she wears cut-off blue-jean shorts because her hips have never recovered from delivering Cricket.

And I don't want to see Charlie Fox after all these years.

Say so, says Cricket.

Ha, Poe says. You can't say so. You can't say so, because it's just a dinner. It's just a gol-rammed dinner with them winking at each other and arranging seats and disappearing to leave us alone. Why does she do this to me? I'm an adult. I can get my own dates.

I know, says Cricket.

I'm my own gol-rammed person.

You're fuming, says Cricket.

This is what it was like to grow up with your grandmother. She was always trying to run my life. I'm going to put my foot down.

Outside the window, the surface of the lake ripples, and the leaves of the birch trees turn over and back, silvery. Cricket stretches out on the bed. A clear plastic shower curtain, spattered with purple paint, covers the white chenille spread.

You're always lying down, says Poe.

No, I'm not.

If you're not going to read you should be outside, doing something. It's a beautiful day. That, or pick up a brush and help me paint.

Down the hall, past Alton in the living room, sleeping, past Ruby and Vi in the kitchen, chatting, through the screened-in porch and out into the front yard with its eight granite boulders in near jumping distance of each other. Alton says that an angel flew over New Hampshire and dropped a bag of granite, and that's why you can't dive in any of the lakes.

In Cricket's game, the boulders are heaven, and the grass, which needs mowing, is hell. Or the boulders are earth and the grass is hell and heaven is the air between boulders when she jumps. Three jumps are easy and one is hard and four are impossible, though on two of the four impossible jumps Cricket can just reach the next rock with her toes, so on those jumps she's not fully in hell.

Careful, says Vi from the kitchen window. Her voice sounds closer, through the screen, than it is.

Cricket lies down in hell, on her stomach. Across the road a policeman opens the trunk of a cruiser and slams it shut. It's the tiny lakefront station, and there are only ever two police cruisers around at a time. Cricket looks at the grass and how perfect and green it is, spears and points, jagged ends where it has been torn or chewed. It's so perfect that after a while of looking at it, she begins to feel sorry for how it's going to turn brown and die in a few months, with no one to remember how beautiful it is but her. She knows that this is the kind of thing that Poe means when she says Cricket is melodramatic.

What are you doing out there, says Vi from the window.

Nothing, Cricket says. Ma'am.

THE NIGHT BEFORE the dinner with Charlie Fox, Poe wakes up swearing so loud out on the porch that Cricket, sleeping on the couch inside, wakes up, too. Poe's using words she's never said aloud before, words she won't repeat at breakfast, in front of Cricket and Alton, that she will only whisper to Vi, later in the day, and will again refuse to repeat at dinner with Charlie Fox, saying three times that she won't repeat them, even though no one has asked her to.

Alton serves food. Three quiches, crusts baked with so much lard they crumble like sand in your mouth. Vi has always been a wonderful cook, and she's kept her looks like no other woman he's seen. She looks better than the women on television, even. But he is not just thinking this, he is thinking himself thinking this, which feels empty, and all the more empty because he would have expected to feel otherwise, proud, or fond, or something, after all this time.

Still, he's skillful with a pie server and keeps each wedge intact except one, which he graciously takes for himself.

You act like a man who's done this before, says Charlie Fox.

All my life, says Alton, all my life. And everyone laughs.

The funny part about the dream, Poe continues, is that I wake up and they've brought someone in across the street. Two cops and this drunk who's going on at the top of his lungs, the same as I was in my dream.

Poe has tied a pale blue scarf around her neck, and she fiddles with the ends.

I didn't hear a thing, says Vi. I sleep through just about everything.

That's the truth, says Alton.

I didn't hear that either, says Cricket. I just heard you.

Poe gives her a tight little smile.

Charlie sleepwalks, says Ruby. Once I caught him just about to pee into an armchair, thinking he'd found the bathroom. Remember that?

I was trying to forget, says Charlie. He's very fair-haired, just beginning to go gray, which has given his handsomeness a new edge. Poe catches his eye and they grimace at each other.

Alton gives Cricket a sip of his red wine, and she tries it because it's in the Bible. Everyone laughs when her face puckers up.

AFTER DINNER, Charlie starts to go out for cigarettes and can't find his keys.

Oh, no, says Vi. She and Ruby are at the sink, doing dishes. Poe has put a Chet Baker album on the turntable and is lighting candles in the living room.

Did you check the ignition? asks Ruby.

Yes, Mother.

Under the front seat? asks Poe, reentering the kitchen with a little dancing in her hips.

Yup, says Charlie, and the backseat and under all the seats and all around the car.

Pockets? asks Ruby.

Charlie doesn't answer her.

Alton walks through the screened-in porch to the door, turns on the outside light, and looks around the stoop.

They could be anywhere, Charlie says. Before dinner he and Poe and Alton and Cricket had walked in the woods, down to the lake, and up the street a half-mile to where a new cabin was going in.

Alton retrieves his two industrial flashlights from the pantry and tries them out, though he knows the batteries are fresh. What more does he have to do with his time, nowadays, than to keep up with these things?

We should split up, Charlie says, looking right at Poe. He takes her elbow as they move out the door, and Ruby and Vi start to whisper. Poe, who has managed to refresh her lipstick without anyone seeing her, turns her head to give them a look, *shut up,* but she might be a tiny bit drunk, and the look turns into a smile.

Cricket follows Alton into the woods, holding on to his belt loops to keep behind him on the path twenty yards left of the lake.

Alton shines the light back and forth in front of him. The air is rich with the throaty sounds of frogs. Where the path winds closer to the lake, the croaking stops and then starts up louder when Alton and Cricket pass, like they're a new topic and all the frogs want to weigh in.

Alton tells Cricket about frog gigging, how you shine the light right at the frog's eyes so it won't move, and then you stick it with a gig, which is a long stick with a tiny pitchfork on the end. Then you put the frog in a bag for later, when you'll fry its legs to eat.

They cut down to the lake and Alton whispers, look now, and shines the light into the swampy part where the water meets the land.

It seems to be all frogs and no distinguishable single frog at the same time. Thin parts and beefy parts, and necks throbbing. In the light, they aren't even green. They're gray. Then the frogs become individual frogs, little and big ones, and Alton points out a big one with the feet of a little one sticking out of its mouth, like the little one jumped in head first by mistake and is waiting for someone to come along and pull him back out.

A ways off in the dark, Charlie Fox's voice comes low and murmuring, the words hard to make out. Poe laughs.

We're not going to find those keys, says Alton.

After a time, Poe laughs again, and then her voice is loud, slipping wild and gulpy over the water, telling what she ends up telling everyone about Cricket's father, can't help herself. Saying, not only is he a prophet, mind you, as if that's not enough.

Laughing, laughing. Charlie Fox laughing too but guarded against a possible shifting. Poe saying he's not only a prophet, but that had it not been for her, for her womanly ways and late-blossoming bookish beauty, Cricket's father believes he would have been Christ the second time around. Jesus H. Fucking Christ, she says, each syllable louder and more resounding across the water.

Isn't that rich? says Poe. There's even a word for it, for people coming back from over there, thinking they're from the Bible. Some syndrome.

The frogs have stopped.

Is he crazy? Charlie says.

Well, I don't know, says Poe. Let me think about that one. Of course he's crazy. Or else he's picked the world's most creative reason to leave me.

Hey, Charlie says. Hey, while Poe's laughter loses control.

Cricket stops walking. She tries to hear what else her mother says, but it doesn't sound like words. Then she stops trying to hear, but she still can. A soft moan, a short, helpless giggle.

Alton turns off the flashlight and stoops in front of her. Katy-did, he whispers, climb up piggyback before you're too big and I'm too old.

Cricket hugs tight with her legs and arms, and to Alton she feels like part of the forest that has wound its way onto him, more like tree roots than limbs, more bony than she was last year, grasping. The only child of his only child. If he could explain anything at all to her, he would, but for now he just cups her knees and hoists her higher on his back, ignoring the warning pain that twinges up from his tailbone. The frogs start up again behind them, and in the dark Alton picks their way back to the house, whistling loudly, over a path he knows by heart.

The Long Game

PRISCILLA'S FATHER comes to visit unannounced and buys her golf shoes, tight Guess? jeans, and a steak, medium rare. She pushes the pink plastic "medium rare" marker into the coin pocket of her jeans and forgets about it until the day after he dies, several months later, when she will find the thing on the floor of her closet, a tiny pink spear between shoes. It's cancer, but he tells Priscilla it's a cold that just hangs on. He looks about the same as when she saw him the year before, handsome, with a broad face and square jaw. Priscilla's mother, Wanda, says she married him because he looked like Pat Boone, which in hindsight was a very stupid reason. She says conventionally handsome men should come with disaster kits.

It's January in Kentucky, when the weather makes a person feel edgy and damp. At home, afterward, Priscilla shrugs out of Wanda's good tan trench coat, borrowed for the occasion. She is fifteen, slightly acned, slightly overweight. She has recently begun trying to straighten her posture to a *regal bearing*—her mother's advice, which she takes only when her mother's not around. Around her mother she is careful to slump.

"Are you okay?" Wanda asks, hugging Priscilla as if she's been gone a week instead of a few hours. Wanda's face is blotchy, her eyes small and red from crying, which is automatic every time Priscilla sees her father. Wanda has managed not to be in the same room with Frank during the decade since divorce court.

"Of course I'm okay," Priscilla says.

"How did he seem?"

"Fine," Priscilla says, with the particular brand of scorn that has prompted Wanda to worry aloud that Priscilla is becoming a difficult person to like.

Wanda grips Priscilla's shoulders and holds her at arm's length. She kneels before Priscilla and looks up into her face. "It's okay," she says, giving Priscilla a little shake for emphasis. "We're okay, you and me. We do what we have to do, don't we?"

"What are you talking about?" Priscilla says, shrugging off the hands.

Wanda breathes deeply, taking air into her diaphragm, as she has explained to Priscilla, so that her lungs are used to full capacity. She learned this from singing in the church choir. Then she breathes out. She stands up. "Was it good to see him?" she asks, and her voice is even and polite, like Priscilla is someone else's child who has had dinner with someone else's ex-husband.

"I guess," says Priscilla, heading down the hallway to her bedroom.

"Does he seem well?" Wanda calls after her.

"I guess," says Priscilla, and closes her bedroom door. In her closet she keeps a file folder of her father's holiday cards. On the inside of the file folder she logs the dates and descriptions of their visits. Tonight she writes, *went to Sizzler, cold out,* and *scoliosis,* which she claimed to have after he told her not to worry about sitting up quite so straight. And when she had tried to just sit, not too straight and not slumped, either, he'd said, "Forget it," knowing and disgusted, as if Wanda were a smell that could begin emanating from Priscilla at any time.

IN MARCH A BOY named Cecil begins to call Priscilla every night. Usually she is allowed to talk to him only ten minutes, but tonight is Wednesday and her mother has gone to prayer meeting. On his stereo Cecil is playing Pink Floyd's *The Wall* for Priscilla, which she has heard before, on the radio. She lies back rigid on her bed, pressing the hard plastic to her ear in case Cecil decides to say anything, and also listening for her mother's car in the driveway. Her yearbook is open to last year's sophomore class. Cecil's smile is large and wet and brutal, and his stick-straight hair hangs over one eye.

"You have a body just like Crystal Cooper's," Cecil says, his voice popping into her ear over the swelling orchestra. Crystal Cooper, cheerleader, turns back handsprings the length of the gym floor during pep rallies at school. Under five feet, she is a miniature Amazon, each thigh bulging like a small round dog.

"Untrue," says Priscilla.

"It's a compliment," says Cecil. "You have the body of the most popular girl in school. I could be with Crystal Cooper right now if I wanted to. That's what's so great about this whole thing. I could have Crystal Cooper—she still likes me—but I'm into you."

"Oh, thanks," Priscilla says, trying not to like the comment but liking it anyway. "How can I ever repay you?"

"You could go with me," Cecil says. "I've asked you a million times."

"I'm not allowed. I already told you." Wanda has explained that it's never a good idea to give in; when a man gets what he wants, he loses interest. She also says that in relationships one person always cares more than the other, and that if you find yourself in that position, you should make sure never to let it show.

"And yet, you're nuts about me," Cecil says. "Maybe someday we'll even—oh my God, kiss. I might even—oh my God, get to kiss my puritan girlfriend." The headlights of Wanda's car in the driveway glint through Priscilla's vertical blinds.

"I'm not puritan," Priscilla says. "I'm saying good-bye now. Good-bye." In approximately one minute and fifteen seconds, Wanda moves from the car to the side door of the house, and down the hall to the closed door of Priscilla's room, where she tries the doorknob before knocking. Priscilla has spread out her chemistry homework, switched on her radio to the fuzzy classics on 90.1, and slid her year-book back into the bookcase; but she has forgotten to un-lock her door.

"Priscilla?" Wanda's voice turns flat against the hollow wood. Priscilla crosses the small room and opens the door as quickly as possible—the knob unlocks with turning—and Wanda stumbles in. "Oh, you're right there. I didn't hear you. I don't understand why you have to keep your door locked as if people are going to come barging in."

"Like you?"

"Oh, give me a break, I'm your mother. You shouldn't be doing anything in here you don't want me to see any-way." Wanda's brown, not-a-strand-of-gray hair, earlier shellacked into a French twist, is sagging over her ears in stiff wings. "I would love to do something different with my hair," she has told Priscilla, "but my facial features are classic and this is a timeless style. Just like the bob."

"I don't like surprises," Priscilla says. She throws her-self across the bed, lying on her stomach, and picks up her pencil.

"Really? What happened to my little girl who liked sur-prises? I miss her."

Priscilla flips two pages in her chemistry book, pretend-ing to read.

"Homework?" Wanda says.

Priscilla copies a problem from the book onto her paper and doesn't answer. She is trying to train Wanda not to ask obvious questions. Wanda leans against the door-jamb, wearing one of the professional ensembles she makes herself. It looks like a suit of separates—white blouse, navy skirt and fitted jacket—but really everything's connected in one piece. The blouse is only the front of a blouse. Wanda keeps talking because, Priscilla thinks, Wanda does not know when to stop, does not seem to know when Priscilla wants to be left alone: How was your day? *Fine.* Anything happen at school? *No.* Nothing happened? I find that hard to believe. *I went to my classes.* And? *And I came home.* Learn anything interesting?

And when Priscilla looks up, Wanda has inclined her head as if she is ready to hear something interesting. Priscilla lays her pencil on the bedspread as if it is a very sharp instrument she doesn't want to be holding in her hand. "Nothing exciting happened at school. Nothing ever does."

Wanda steps out of her navy pumps and walks to Priscilla's dresser, where she begins to put scattered hot rollers back in their case. "How was *your* day, Mom?" she says. "Did you find that file for your boss? The one he yelled at you about yesterday? Why, yes I did, and since it was exactly where it belonged, I suspect he found it in his briefcase, where I told him it might be, and then filed it so he wouldn't have to admit he lost it. Gosh, Mom, I'm sorry things are rocky at work." Wanda snaps shut the hot-roller case and stares into the mirror at Priscilla on the bed behind her. Priscilla raises her eyebrows and stares back. "Mom," Wanda continues, "since Wednesdays you get home late, I thought I'd make dinner tonight, just to help out. It's all ready in the stove. Doesn't it smell good?" Priscilla blinks, holds her stare. Wanda shifts her lower jaw to one side and shakes her head, just barely. "I always ask you about your day. I want to know how your day went, and sometimes it would be nice if you asked how my day went, that's all."

"You don't have to ask me how my day went," Priscilla says. "There's never anything to say anyway."

"There's always something to say, Priscilla. It's called making conversation. The women in our family are famous for it."

"Then go talk to one of them."

"These difficult teen years are so much fun for me, you know that?" Wanda walks to the door. "I just enjoy your thoughtful spirit. But I love you, even if you don't love me."

Then she is gone, the door left open. Priscilla gets up to close it and calls, "I love you, okay?" but Wanda just flutters her hand behind her back and heads to the kitchen to make dinner. Once, Wanda had made a point not to speak to Priscilla except when absolutely necessary from a Wednesday to a Friday, and then she'd cried and yelled for the whole weekend because Priscilla hadn't noticed. *I'm sorry,* Priscilla had said, genuinely surprised. She'd thought it was peaceful. *You didn't even care,* said Wanda. *I might as well be invisible.* But then Priscilla cleaned the bathroom without being asked, which was, Wanda had told her some time before, one little way she could be considerate. Afterward Wanda had cried again, and thanked her.

At dinner Priscilla and Wanda sit at one side of a scarred wood folding table, pushed up against double windows. It's dark out. Their house is the last in a row of brick ranch houses that ends in a large cow pasture. When you look out the double windows in the daytime, you can't see another house—it's fields on fields until the road, some two miles away, but you can't see the road, either. When the grass is low and the cows aren't around, Priscilla drives golf balls into the expanse. She's the best golfer on the school team, though few people at her school realize there even is a golf team.

Tonight it's just the dim reflection of Priscilla and Wanda and dinner: one boiled hot dog each, on a slice of whole wheat bread with a strip of ketchup, spinach from a frozen box, boiled and divided into two limp wads. It's nearly nine.

"Is this going to be enough for you?" Wanda asks. "Did you snack?"

Priscilla picks up her hot dog. The bread is instantly soggy with ketchup, and her fingers make four red indentations.

"There's all those carrots and celery sticks I made up in the crisper. They're good for you. Whenever you get hungry, you just fill up on those."

"Okay."

"Did you eat some of those after school?"

"I made some oatmeal."

They look at each other in the dark window. Wanda has tucked a paper towel into the neck of her ensemble dress. Priscilla wears her brown hair in one high ponytail. It's still curly from the hot rollers that morning. Large silver metal peace signs dangle from her pierced ears.

"I don't know how you make it through the day in those earrings," says Wanda. "My lobes would be sore. Aren't you afraid they'll catch on something and tear your lobes?" Priscilla puts down her hot dog and takes out her earrings, laying them in a small pile on the table at the head of her plate. "I'm not saying you have to take them out, honey, I'm just saying I couldn't wear them because I'd be afraid they'd catch on something and tear."

Priscilla shudders and pinches her earlobes between her thumbs and fingers. "Could you just not say that?"

"What, *tear?*"

Priscilla shudders again.

Wanda laughs. "It's just a word, honey. You have such a vivid imagination." Wanda finishes her hot dog and picks at her spinach. "This isn't such an exciting dinner. You're getting to the age where you really could start taking care of dinner once in a while. It would be good training for you."

"I don't need training," Priscilla says, "and I have things to do."

"You wouldn't be so busy if you didn't spend so much time on the phone. I was trying to reach you from work."

"Rosemary wanted to know about chemistry."

Wanda grimaces in the window. "Rosemary. I wish you would spend more time with Jonna instead. She always speaks to me in church." Once when Rosemary invited Priscilla over and Wanda asked to talk to her mother on the phone, Rosemary said that her mother didn't exactly live there right then, but that next week she probably would.

"Rosemary is a nice person. She's my best friend."

"She is not your best friend, she is a school friend. And I know she is a nice person. Anyone else call? What's-his-name?"

Priscilla shrugs.

"Cecil, right? Cecil? How long did you two stay on the phone?"

"I hardly even talked to him."

"That boy likes you."

"We're *friends*."

"What about your father?" asks Wanda. "Have you heard from him?"

"No," says Priscilla, and she makes an ugly, tolerant face to let Wanda know how stupid that question is. He calls on Christmas, her birthday, Father's Day, and the Fourth of July. He has said she can call him collect anytime she wants to, has asked her to, even. Whenever she does think of calling, every reason she thinks of seems stupid.

"That visit," Wanda says, "I don't know. Something was strange about his eyes."

"Oh, really," Priscilla says. "When did you even get a chance to see his eyes?"

"Didn't you tell me he had a cold while he was here?"

"No."

"And before, didn't you tell me he had the flu when he called for your birthday? And last Christmas, too, he had a cold or something, didn't he?"

"I don't remember." Priscilla shovels all her spinach into her mouth. Cheeks bulging, she chews and chews.

"I have a bad feeling about it," Wanda says.

Priscilla takes her plate to the sink and runs water on it. Then she opens the freezer for a spoonful of ice cream.

"This is how the weight goes on, Priscilla. These bites that no one keeps track of. A bite here, a bite there, it all adds up. Listen to me. I've been one hundred and fifteen pounds for twenty years now. And I think your father's cancer is back, that's what I think. It's not like him to come visit for no reason like that."

"Maybe he missed me," Priscilla says.

"It's not like him," Wanda says again. "I'll bet he knows something's wrong."

"You don't even know him," Priscilla says.

"I lived with him twelve years. I guess I know a thing or two. All I'm saying is, don't be surprised if you find out he's sick. I'm not trying to scare you. I just think you should prepare yourself." Wanda sighs through her nose. "He hasn't been the best father, I know," and here Wanda's voice becomes tentative, takes on her special, post-prayer-meeting waver, "but you have a heavenly father who will never let you down."

Priscilla spoons more ice cream into her mouth, and her teeth throb.

"Okay, well, just think about that," Wanda says. "And that's enough ice cream."

At school, Priscilla and Rosemary wait by Priscilla's locker for Cecil and his friends to pass. Priscilla is wearing her tight new jeans, over Wanda's protests.

"Look busy," Priscilla whispers, when she sees him

coming down the hall. "Don't let it seem like we're waiting for him."

Rosemary reaches into the top part of the locker and looks down at her with gray eyes rimmed above and below with teal eyeliner, lashes crusted with black mascara. "What's wrong with waiting for him? He's your boyfriend, so you wait for him."

"No, you don't. You can't let men think you just wait around for them."

"He's so cute," Rosemary says. "You don't even act like you like him."

"Oh, please," Priscilla says. First, she arranges her books in the order she will need them: algebra, chemistry, English, English workbook. When she feels Cecil standing behind her, she arranges them again, backwards, before turning around.

"Hey," says Cecil, flipping his straight shock of hair out of his eye.

"Hey," says Priscilla. She raises her eyebrows and does not smile. Cecil raises his eyebrows back.

Cecil's friend, Dwight, punches Rosemary on the arm and Rosemary holds up a hand, rings on every finger, inches from Dwight's narrow face. "Don't even," she says.

"Easy on Dwight," says Cecil. "He had quite a night last night, didn't you, Dwight?" Cecil grins at everyone except, it seems, Priscilla, and so Priscilla doesn't look at him. She throws her hip to the side and cocks her head. Her new jeans are cutting into her stomach.

"Dwight got sauced," Cecil says. Then he turns to

Dwight and mumbles something. Priscilla stands there with her hip out, tapping her foot.

"Your girlfriend's pissed, man," Dwight says.

"Hey," Cecil says, elbowing Priscilla. "What's the problem?"

"No problem."

He turns to Dwight and pushes him. "You said 'pissed,' man, and she doesn't talk like that. She's pissed because you said 'pissed.' Priscilla is a very good girl."

"I say 'pissed,'" Priscilla says. "Please, I say 'pissed' all the time."

"Then what, you uptight?"

"No, are you? Anything you want to say to me?"

"No." Cecil looks confused.

"No," Priscilla says. "It didn't really seem like it." Other kids jostle by them in the hallway and someone calls, deep, *Hey Cecil*. Uptight isn't good, but Priscilla does not know what to say. What do other girls say when they aren't acting mad? A lump like pie dough has formed in her stomach. "This is stupid," she says, turning around and slamming her locker closed. "I'm outta here."

As soon as Priscilla lets herself in the side door at home, the phone rings. "My girlfriend's mad at me," Cecil says.

"Shut up," says Priscilla, but there's a tiny smile in it.

"My girlfriend burned me in front of the buds."

"Your girlfriend?" Priscilla says. "At school you don't even talk to me. You stand there and talk to everyone but me."

"You want to talk? Talk. What do you want to talk about? You're very serious, Priscilla. You should lighten up. You ever had a boyfriend before?"

Priscilla slams her books on the kitchen table and stretches the phone cord to the refrigerator. "Of course. I've had tons of boyfriends. And don't tell me to lighten up. I've got a lot on my mind."

"So do I."

"I mean a *lot* on my mind." In the fridge, in the Tupperware crisper, bite-sized carrot and celery sticks in water float and bump around her fingers like fish.

"So tell me," Cecil says. "I'm your boyfriend, so let's *talk* about it. I've got a lot on my mind, too."

"Well does your dad have cancer?"

"No, but my grandmother does. She's going to die."

"So is my dad, probably," says Priscilla, but she feels deflated. Also, she wonders if it might be true, now that she's said it out loud. She crunches into a carrot.

"What kind of cancer?"

"I'm not sure," Priscilla says. "Just cancer. He had it a long time ago in his neck or something, but that was before I was born. My mom thinks he has it again."

"My grandmother has lung cancer," Cecil says. "She has an oxygen tank, and she is definitely going to die before your dad dies. She's in the hospital. Is your dad?"

"I don't think so. He might be. He lives in Florida. His name is Frank. I live with my mom."

"My dad's name is Clyde and my mom's name is Bonnie, get it? Now you tell me something else."

"Um," Priscilla says. "I play golf. I can drive the ball 200 yards."

"Wow," Cecil says. "That's far. That's far out. Get it?"

"Yes," says Priscilla. "Ha ha." They are silent. Priscilla listens to him breathing. In her head she counts to thirteen. "One time I choked," she says, remembering. "On a butterscotch candy."

"You choked? You mean you almost choked. If you choked you'd be dead."

He's teasing, and Priscilla is relieved that it's time to act mad again. "Whatever you say, Cecil," she says. "Only don't ask about me if you don't want to know."

"Priscilla's pissed again. Excuse me, Priscilla's ticked off."

"I'm pissed, and I have to get off the phone. My mom calls to see if it's busy."

After she hangs up, Priscilla opens the freezer. The ice cream is plain vanilla, the cheap store-brand kind with a plastic additive that Priscilla heard about on television. She sticks her face into the freezer and closes her eyes and wonders if she is now a girl whose father is dying. It sounds more important than it feels. Her cheeks turn cold and heavy, and she can feel her eyes moving against her eyelids. When she forgets about everything but how it feels to put your head into a freezer, she shivers and pulls her head back out.

She collects her driver and cleats and bucket and heads out to the backyard, where it's cool but not cold. A small clump of brown and white cows has gathered near the fence by the neighbor's backyard, but Priscilla sends a few whistling over their heads and soon they are gone. Priscilla is secretly proud of cows for how fast they can move when they want to. She should stretch, but she doesn't. She works her feet into her stance and sends ball after ball high into the air. For this afternoon her goal is clearing the creek, which is her 200-yard mark. People do not usually believe she can do this, consistently, at least, until she shows them. She does the usual stuff—thinking speed, not power, keeping her head down, shortening her backswing when she feels off—but her real secret is the rubber body. Each time she tees up, she imagines her body is made of solid, gymnasium-floor rubber, hard enough to keep shape during routine use, but with enough give to absorb maximum impact. During her backswing, while her hips and shoulders do everything she's taught them to do without her having to try, she focuses on the ball; instead of feeling the club head move toward the ball, she feels the ball moving toward the club head, whistling like a missile. The *thuck* of contact travels up the shaft to her hands and down her arms and then is taken up by every cell in her, like every cell has a tiny stomach that has received a tiny blow from a tiny fist. Each drive leaves her shaken, but then her body readjusts. Her short game is terrible, so she rarely wins, but her long game makes other coaches drop their jaws.

When the bucket is empty, Priscilla climbs over the barbed-wire fence. In the field the grass and weeds have been chewed or flattened, packed into the hard, damp Kentucky clay. Hiking toward the creek, breathing deeply, the chill air goes all the way up her nose, a clean feeling. The sky glows orange and pink as the sun sinks. The cows, over a rise in land just out of sight, are mooing. *Lowing,* Priscilla thinks. When she was little, her father made her memorize different cow names, but all she remembers are Black Angus, which are, of course, black. She takes a running start and leaps across the ditch. Most of the golf balls are visible, and Priscilla collects them quickly. In the deeper rough she kicks through the grass and keeps her eyes sharp. What she doesn't find now she will find later, though she worries a little about whether or not a cow can swallow a golf ball. Before heading back, she stands with her eyes closed, feeling the expanse of sky and land, smelling the cold field and the cows and the creek. This gives her insides an ache, like they recognize something. *This is what girls do when their fathers die,* she says to herself, but really she does this all the time. Now, though, she has to wonder about the possibility of significance. She likes the idea that when she dies, her body will dissolve into the earth and feed it. She wonders if her father believes this, too, wonders if it's what he's hoping for.

From 200 yards behind her, Wanda calls. She's at the barbed-wire fence in her work clothes, waving hard, maybe even hopping a little. Priscilla waves back and watches to see if Wanda wants something, but Wanda just stands at the fence a moment longer before making her way back across the lawn to the house.

"A glory sky," Wanda says when Priscilla enters the kitchen from the back door. "You cross the Midwest with the South and that's what you get. Don't you love that sky? It's really something, Priscilla."

"It's nice," Priscilla says, but now she loves the sky a little bit less. She can't help it. It's hard to feel anything much when Wanda is in the room, using up all the feeling.

"The flat, cool expanse of the Midwest," Wanda says. "The warm, rolling hills of the South." She makes a flat expanse and then a rolling-hill motion with her hand. Unexpectedly, Priscilla enjoys watching her do this. She remembers flat fields from driving through Indiana, rows of crops so long and straight they made you dizzy, speeding by. At the kitchen counter, Wanda is adding ingredients to a bowl for pizza dough. She has taken off her heels, and Priscilla is taller by two inches. Wanda pinches salt and baking powder without having to measure; she makes a bowl shape in the flour for the yeast and water. The pizza crust will be thin and crispy, and the thought of it makes Priscilla's mouth water.

"Do you remember when I choked on that butterscotch candy?" Priscilla asks. "When I was two?"

"In the Berea duplex? Where'd you get butterscotch candy?"

"I don't know," Priscilla says. Wanda hands Priscilla the mixing bowl. Priscilla turns on the oven, sets the dough on the back burner, and covers the bowl with the dish towel while Wanda washes her hands.

"It could have been one of those girls I used to have stay with you," Wanda says, "but they were pretty sensible girls most of the time."

"I don't remember who gave it to me," says Priscilla, "but Daddy held me upside down over the toilet and shook me until it came out."

"Really?" says Wanda. "I can't believe I don't remember that. Could be he didn't tell me."

"Remember when the dog bit me?"

"I don't believe I'll ever forget that one," Wanda says.

"It put its paws on my shoulders," Priscilla says, "and then I was sitting on the couch and I put my hands up to my face and there was blood."

Wanda shakes her head and covers her eyes with her hand. "I was out shopping, and that friend of your father's brought that dog over and they left you in the house with it."

"Just for a minute," Priscilla says.

"Your father was shaking when he told me," Wanda says. "It really shook him up so I didn't even yell, but I didn't think I'd ever forgive him. I'd never seen your father so scared. He kept saying, 'her face, her face,' and his own face was white as a sheet. I had to stop him from shooting that dog, but I didn't want to. I don't like guns, but I wanted him to shoot that dog."

"I stepped on its hurt paw, though," Priscilla says. "I didn't mean to. It wasn't really the dog's fault."

"There's nipping," says Wanda, "and then there's biting. Some dogs are just bad dogs."

"Cecil has two bloodhounds," Priscilla says. "Hazel and Homer. He has a picture of them in his locker. They have the wrinkly faces."

"Tell me about this Cecil," Wanda says, the tiniest bit of teasing creeping into her voice.

Priscilla smiles. She can't help it. "What do you mean? He's just Cecil."

"Not a boyfriend?"

"No," says Priscilla, still smiling.

"Well he certainly keeps in touch. Maybe this Cecil and I should have a chat." Wanda's voice is still teasing, but something else is there, too, and it makes Priscilla want to snatch back the name Cecil so that Wanda can't say it anymore.

"Please," Priscilla says. "He's just in my class and he has these dog pictures in his locker."

"Hazel and Homer. What interesting names."

And now Priscilla wants those names back, too. She sees the Polaroid taped inside Cecil's locker door, sees the dogs' eyes red from the flash, sees Cecil standing there when he showed them to her, pointing to one then the other, naming their names.

"Wonder how he came up with those names," Wanda says, "your boyfriend."

"How should I know?" Priscilla says, backing out of the kitchen. "He's not my boyfriend. We're not *friendly,* I said."

"That's not what it sounds like to me," Wanda says in the impossible, teasing voice that doesn't mean teasing at all. It means that now Wanda will float like a gas into all the space in Priscilla's head around Cecil, crowding her thoughts until she's ready to bang her skull against a rock.

————

Rosemary has first lunch, and Priscilla has second, so she has to sit at a table of kids from the youth group at church. Priscilla rarely attends youth group, but the table is a place to sit. If she lingers in her classroom, stops by the bathroom, and lets people cut in front of her in the lunch line, she will miss the holding of hands and prayer chant, after which some of the other tables always clap, and during which at least three voices yell at them to shut up, which the Christian table bears proudly as a sign of persecution.

Cecil sits at the other end of the cafeteria, at a table of boys who are marginally popular. The few girls who sit there are girlfriends, cheerleaders, mostly. Crystal Cooper sat there until she and Cecil broke up. Cecil's table doesn't make fun of the Christian table. They can afford to be generous, is how Priscilla imagines they think about it. Or else they just don't notice.

Priscilla hopes Cecil hasn't realized they have the same lunch. Once he knows, they will either have to sit together, or go on not sitting together and be aware of it. She cannot imagine sitting at Cecil's table. The girls there all live in the subdivisions around the golf course, where she competes. From the third, seventh, and fifteenth tee, Priscilla has seen the weedless backyards where they practice cheers or work on their suntans. Even sweaty, these girls seem cleaner than Priscilla has ever felt in her life.

Her friend at the Christian table is Jonna, who is tall and hunched and pining for a boy named Chad. "He wants to do inner-city missions this summer, and so do I," Jonna informs her today, nodding toward where Chad sits at the guys' end of the table.

Chad is blond and slight, with a fuzz of new mustache. "That'll be good," Priscilla says. "I predict romance."

"Thanks," Jonna says. "I heard you're going with Cecil." She turns her head to look at Cecil's table.

"Please don't do that," Priscilla says. She opens her Tupperware sandwich container. The sandwich looks normal enough, from the outside. Often it is normal—plain bologna and a few hunks of cheddar, or pink tuna fish, without mayo, mixed with a chopped dill pickle. Today, though, when Priscilla peels back the top piece of whole wheat bread, she finds that Wanda has made the chicken-part sandwich. It's leftovers from Sunday's Crock-Pot chicken, all the little parts, the almond-shaped pieces of dark meat, the squiggly brown things that aren't meat but that can't be entirely picked away. Veins, or tendons. Congealed fat in the space between pieces has formed a clear jelly. Wanda has sliced off cold pats of butter with which she lines each slice of bread. Jonna chews her bite of BLT and sips from a foil-packed juice drink. When she sees the sandwich, she stops chewing.

"Why don't you tell her you want something different?" Jonna says.

"She won't do it," says Priscilla. "She eats the same thing. She makes her lunch the same time she makes mine." Priscilla carefully picks all the chicken off her bread, and with a plastic cafeteria knife she spreads the softened butter pats. She likes bread and butter, and even though this tastes like bread and chicken-part butter, the consistency is at least bearable. When Wanda asks if she ate her sandwich, she will say that she gagged on the chicken jelly, and Wanda will say she is being hyperbolic.

"Maybe she doesn't look at it," Jonna says, covering the small mound of unnamable chicken with a stiff cafeteria napkin. "Maybe you should buy a school lunch."

"Saving money is kind of the point," says Priscilla. "For college."

"It's only a dollar," Jonna says. "You can borrow one, but I need it back."

"That's okay."

Jonna looks toward Cecil's table again. "Didn't Cecil used to go with that short cheerleader? Crystal something? Because she's sitting with him. She wasn't before, but she moved from her table and now she's sitting with him."

Priscilla swallows a mouthful of bread and butter. She is conscious of her stomach as distinct, suddenly, from any other organ. It flips over in a kind of terror, but Priscilla just shakes her head and narrows her eyes as if she is only very, very angry. "Don't look," she says. "Tell me what's happening, but don't look."

"They're talking, she's talking, oh and now he's got his arm around her."

"Don't look," Priscilla says again.

"Okay," Jonna says after a minute. "Now she's leaving. She's wearing her cheerleader skirt and she's leaving with another cheerleader and he's waving, or you know, not waving, really, but lifting up his finger from the table."

"Well, I don't care," says Priscilla. At the end of the table, Chad is looking at her, mouthing "hi." He says hi to her every time she goes to church. She raises her index finger from the table and nods her head, the exact motion she imagines Cecil has just performed. Jonna takes it in.

"Chad never says 'hi' first," Jonna whispers. "Do you like him? Because if you do, I would really appreciate it if you told me."

"Have you ever had a boyfriend?" Priscilla asks her.

"No."

"Well then you're lucky."

AFTER FOURTH PERIOD she doesn't go to her locker, just to make Cecil wonder. After fifth period he doesn't show up at hers. After school she doesn't see him anyway, because she is embarrassed to be riding the bus while he rides with friends who drive. On the way home Priscilla sits by a grimy window, teeth clenched. As she walks up the hill to her house she hisses to herself. *Have a nice lunch, Cecil? See an old friend, Cecil? Using me to make her jealous, Cecil? Crystal Cooper with her back handsprings?* She works herself into a few tears, which run down her face, hot in the cool air. It is a relief to have something to be angry about.

In the house, she turns on the television, then turns it off, then eats a box of crackers, waiting for him to call. She goes into the bathroom to watch herself talk, practicing different ways to say, *have a nice lunch?* Her cheeks are pink and her lips are wide and full and she tries to make a sexy, noncaring face. She imagines making a scene in the hall at school, where she will use the word "fuck" and tell him to never, ever, even think about calling her again. She goes through this scene a couple times until more tears come and her throat hurts from whispering so loudly—even alone in the house she doesn't, for some reason, talk aloud. She can't hear the phone ringing until she stops to wash her face, and when she answers she is out of breath and awkward: "Hello?" and she would like it to sound different, less eager, but it isn't Cecil after all.

It's Denise, her stepmother, saying, "Hi, hon. Is your mom around?"

"She's at work," Priscilla says. "You want to talk to my mom?"

"Yeah, sweetie. How are you doing? You doing okay?" Denise's voice is kinder than usual, though it's always kind because Denise wants Priscilla to like her, and Priscilla does, even though she has tried not to, for her mother's sake.

"I'm okay," Priscilla says. Then: "Is something wrong with my dad?"

"Well, actually, not really," Denise says. "He's pretty sick, I guess."

Priscilla stands in the doorway between the kitchen and the living room. Outside the light is gray from the clouds, and inside it seems as if the air is the same air she has been breathing for months.

"It's good he visited you," Denise continues after a brief silence. "He's very proud of you."

"Okay," Priscilla says, trying to remember what she told him about golf.

"He's always telling the girls, 'Priscilla studies hard and makes good grades. Priscilla is a very good athlete.' He's always saying that."

"I don't study that hard. In some of my classes you can get B's and they count as A's."

"Well, he's very proud anyway," says Denise. "He always tells people he has another daughter."

"It's okay," Priscilla says, because Denise sounds like she's crying.

"I should talk to your mom," Denise says, and Priscilla understands that her father is going to die. Probably soon. She gives Denise the number. "I'll be in touch," Denise tells her. "You're okay, hon?"

"Yes." After hanging up, Priscilla says aloud, "My father is going to die." She speaks as if the words will make her sad. She stands by the phone and waits to start crying again, for the scratchiness in the back of her throat, the squinting up of her eyes. Nothing happens. She thinks of how her father would sometimes say he missed her, and how she would say she missed him, too, but that she hadn't really missed him except when she was very little, right after he left. She has long since forgotten what having an everyday father feels like. The truth is that she isn't sure what to miss anymore, and she doesn't really know how he could know what to miss, either. Perhaps when people talked about things they wished they'd said to loved ones before they died, this was the type of thing they meant. Perhaps this was when people acknowledged to each other that most of the time they spoke they were not saying what they really meant at all. She wonders if this would be anything her father would be interested in hearing before he dies.

When the phone rings again, Priscilla is surprised that she still hopes it is Cecil, at, she thinks, a time like this.

"I'm coming right home," Wanda says, "so we can talk."

"I'm fine," Priscilla says. "You don't have to."

"Of course I'm coming home. We need each other, you and me. Don't try to be tough, Priscilla."

"Whatever you say," Priscilla says, because Wanda hates it when she says this. And when she hangs up, she calls Cecil. Wanda has told her that only a certain type of girl calls a boy, and that boys know this even if they say differently; but at a time like this, Priscilla thinks, none of the rules apply.

"I heard you were back with Crystal Cooper," Priscilla says when Cecil answers.

"What? Oh, hey. Who told you that?"

"So it's true?"

"Not exactly," he says. "Maybe."

"Did you notice I wasn't at my locker?" Priscilla says, and then wishes she hadn't. He was supposed to have asked her where she was so she could act like she just forgot to meet him. She wasn't supposed to let him know she didn't show up on purpose.

"No, I didn't," Cecil says. "I wasn't there, either. I got held up. You're uptight again, I can tell. It's no big deal, Priscilla. I like you, but I will always love Crystal Cooper. We went together for eight months. You won't even say you're going with me."

"Well, I guess that's a good thing, since you love someone else."

"You take things way too seriously, anyway," Cecil says, "and you're kind of a bitch."

"Fuck you," Priscilla says, and it feels like a huge thing to say. "I didn't need this today."

"You started it."

"Fuck," Priscilla says, now crying into the phone. She can't remember the last time she let anyone hear her cry. She almost tells him about her father. Who she's not even crying about, who she can't even, most days, pull up as a picture in her head. Then she could make Cecil sorry for calling her a bitch. Instead, she just says, "Fuck, fuck, fuck."

"I don't get why you're crying. You need to lighten up."

"Don't tell me to lighten up," Priscilla screams into the phone. "Don't you *dare* tell me to lighten up."

"Okay, don't then," Cecil says, his voice too reasonable. "Why are we still on the phone?"

Priscilla hangs up, and like that, it's over. One day things are one way, and the next day things are another way, she tells herself, and it's stupid to cry; but she's crying, anyway, because he won't be calling her anymore and this means something, even at a time like this.

Wanda is on her way home. Priscilla washes her face again and hustles to the backyard with her driver. She tees up, swishes the club head through the grass a couple of times. She looks into the field—no cows—and picks her spot. It's grass like the rest of the field, but there's a slight dip, a deeper color green from the rain. Spring is almost here. Her mind empties of everything except how her body is like rubber. It's as if her brain has moved from her head to her limbs, and her thoughts have all become movements. The first shot is clean and high and perfect. She has heard of blind people who hit a beeping ball, and she tries the next one with her eyes closed, concentrating to allow the ball and the fist-sized club head to pull toward each other like magnets. Another clean shot. The ball soars and drops into the deep green grass with a sweet shush she can almost hear. It happens again and again. It occurs to her that if her father saw her do this, he would have a better idea what to be proud of.

After a time, Wanda's car pulls into the drive. *Don't stop me,* Priscilla thinks. *Please don't stop me.* At the top of her backswing, the car door slams, and she opens her eyes. It throws everything off. She swings anyway, but the club head digs into the ground a foot in front of the tee, with all the force of her momentum. Her body, now just bones and muscle, shakes with the impact, and she stumbles out of her stance. When she looks up, Wanda is picking her way across the lawn in her work heels. In one hand she carries a handkerchief.

"Honey," she calls.

"Just a second," Priscilla says. She swings again at the ball on the tee, eyes open, and duffs it through the barbed wire fence. "Shit," she says. She tees up another ball, too fast—you should never hurry golf—but then Wanda is on her, crying.

"Come inside," Wanda says.

"In a minute."

"I've got some bad news," Wanda says.

"I already know," Priscilla says. She doesn't look at Wanda. She locates her spot in the field and narrows her eyes.

"Honey, stop. Your father's not going to make it." Priscilla lines up behind the tee and settles into her stance. She loosens her arms and lets the club head brush the grass in front of the tee like a gentle pendulum. "He lost consciousness this morning," Wanda says. "He's been sick for a long time. Denise found out he had everything taken care of a long time ago." Priscilla rotates her shoulder where it hurts from driving the club into the ground. She wonders how long Wanda will continue to talk. She knows that saying these words in this way, like on television shows, makes her feel important. "I knew he was sick," Wanda says. "His doctor said he didn't want chemotherapy. He didn't want anyone to know. He kind of gave up." Wanda dabs at her eyes with the handkerchief. "He wasn't a happy man. Come on, now," she says, with renewed authority. "Let's go inside."

"I want to be alone," Priscilla says, keeping her head down, looking at the dimples on the ball. Pick a dimple, was her old method of concentration. Keep your head down, pick a dimple, and then don't move your eyes.

Wanda breathes in—diaphragm—and draws herself up, squaring her shoulders. "Well, you can't," she says, cross. "Your father's dying and I won't let you be alone. Put down the damn golf club."

Priscilla rests the club head lightly on the grass and stares at the golf ball, at the tiny gray dimple she's chosen. If she were small enough, she could curl up in the cool shallow indentation and sleep. When Wanda grabs the shaft of the golf club, Priscilla wrenches it back easily, surprised at her own strength.

"He's been a disappointment," Wanda says. "He hasn't been the best father. Your heavenly father," Wanda begins, then lets it trail away. "But he's your father, after all— Frank, I mean—and he's going to die and you are going to feel this."

"Okay, so why are *you* crying?" Priscilla says. Her voice is calm, like she's asking a question she's genuinely interested in the answer to. She inspects Wanda's eyes. They look raw. They look like someone's traced them with a red pencil.

"I'm sad," Wanda says. "When I'm sad it helps me to cry, and I wish you would."

"You're sad," Priscilla says. "But he's my father, and he's your nothing." Not taking her eyes from her mother's, she winds into her backswing in slow motion.

"He was my husband," Wanda says, making another grab for the club, near Priscilla's face.

Priscilla jerks it out of the way and cocks it behind her head, parallel to the ground. "Stop doing that," she says.

"We were married." Wanda's breath is ragged. "Do you even understand that?"

"We were married," Priscilla says. She takes a few exaggerated breaths.

Something changes in Wanda's face. She has looked worried, in the angry, confused way she gets worried for Priscilla, and now her mouth opens and she looks worried for herself. It is growing dark, and Priscilla leans toward her, curious. Wanda steps back quickly. Her eyes go to the golf club behind Priscilla's head. Priscilla wonders if Wanda thinks she will swing at her. As she's wondering, she feels herself beginning to swing, then stopping—a feint. Wanda steps back again. Once more, and this time Priscilla adds a step toward her. Wanda tenses up her body. The exact thing not to do, Priscilla thinks, if you're expecting a blow. Wanda looks small and scared, and Priscilla is sorry, suddenly, and wants to explain about rubber body. She starts to smile to show she doesn't mean it, and she lowers the club. She loves her mother. But then Wanda's face relaxes and Priscilla can see in it all the words that will follow, the scolding, the understanding, the push to turn Priscilla inside out so that there will be nothing Priscilla can think of that Wanda doesn't already expect.

Priscilla's smile freezes. She hates her mother. She jerks the club back and watches Wanda's face change again, hears her gasp. Priscilla steps forward, Wanda steps back. Priscilla lowers the club, Wanda tries to smile; Priscilla rears the club again, Wanda tenses. The whole thing has become automatic, as if they are opposite ends of a rhythmic pull-toy, edging themselves around the yard. Priscilla feels a queer oneness with the club, the yard, the air, and the body before her that is her mother, and though it seems there is nothing in the world to be accomplished, Priscilla knows she can keep it up for as long as it takes.

Acknowledgments

MANY THANKS TO THE Wallace Stegner program at Stanford, SUNY Albany, Indiana University, the Indiana Arts Council, the Kentucky Council for the Arts, and Headlands Center for the Arts in Marin.

I am grateful for the early support of Josh Gibbons, Marcia Hurlow, Cornelia Nixon, Tony Ardizzone, Brooke Sanderson, Karen Heath, Karri Offstein, Amy Fisher-Lutz, David Mills, Van Khanna, and Jeff Calderone. And for the voices that have kept me going—Julie Orringer, Adam Johnson, Stephanie Harrell, Ed Schwarzchild, Doug Dorst, Ann Williams, Katharine Noel, Caroline Goodwin, Brian Teare, Tamara Guirardo, Jason Brown, and Daniel Orozco. Thanks to my teachers: John L'Heureux, Elizabeth Tallent, and Tobias Wolff. Thanks to Regina Lutz, Charlie Eckstrom, Ingrid Johnson, Sheila Franks, Denise Gunter, Monica Negri, Cheryl Deaner, Nancy Lynch, Tina Pohlman, and Eric Simonoff.

Most of all, thanks to Michelle Blankenship—oldest friend and instigator; ZZ Packer—comrade and confessor; and Nina Pneuman—my mother, librarian extraordinaire, who read to me story upon story.